Arena Stage

BarbarianSpy

FOR LITERARY HEAT

www.BarbarianSpy.com

WARNING: This book is for sale to **ADULT AUDIENCES ONLY**. Contains graphic gay male sex, multiple partners, anal sex, and gay romance and love, all of which may be considered offensive by some readers.

All sexually active characters in this work are at least 18 years of age.

This book is copyright © habu 2014
habu asserts his right to be known as the author of this work.
Published by BarbarianSpy in 2014
Cover design © S Bush 2014
Cover image: Manipulated, Copyright: ostill Shutterstock
ISBN: 978-0-9876093-9-7
All rights reserved

BarbarianSpy
Jindalee St
Toronto, NSW 2283
Australia

Arena Stage

by

habu

CONTENTS

Chapter One: Gil

All of the lions were present now. And, as I would have guessed from his reputation, the king of the jungle was the last to arrive, swirling in with his cute-boy assistant trailing behind him, juggling all of the paraphernalia the "great man" traveled with. I gotta admit that I was disappointed that Creighton Masters lived up to his reputation on first look. In fact, he was even more so. We were gathering in the dimly lit dance practice hall on a gloomy late afternoon, the lights fifteen feet overhead doing little to illuminate the blueprints and note cards strewn across the rickety card table in the middle of the polished hardwood floor.

But once Creighton Masters appeared at the double doors at the far end of the room, bellowing his, "Hi ho, Lenny" and his "Oh no, don't bother to rise, Milo," the room took on a luminance that was astonishing. I smiled when I looked up at the window and saw that the sun had emerged from the clouds over the nation's capital just at that moment, but I didn't discount that "The Master" had planned that for his grand entrance. There was a heavenly choir bursting forth—in my mind, at least.

Leonard Handelsman and Miloslav Cersenka had risen, their faces beaming and broadcasting their pleasure, their feeling of completeness, as Creighton Masters strode down the length of the room toward them, his oversized trench coat flapping about him like angel's wings. Of course they stood in homage; he had told them not to, but he knew they would, and because he had reminded them that it might be called for, they did—for Masters was The Master.

"It's good to see you again, Lenny," Masters nearly bellowed, as he swept his Stetson hat off his head with a flourish and flipped it off to the side, onto the polished hardwood floor. He grabbed for one of the half dozen folding metal chairs haphazardly scattered about, all within ten feet of the card table, and turned it to where its back almost touched the side of the table across from where Handelsman had been seated and to the left of where Cersenka had been sunk into his chair at the table and sat, legs spread and muscled thighs hugging the metal chair seat. With a grand motion of both arms held out wide, Masters motioned for the two to return to their seats, which they did, turning their faces toward Masters as if he was going to deliver a sermon they ached to hear.

Masters turned to Cersenka. "And you are looking very well, Milo."

"Thank you, and you too, Mr. Masters," Cersenka murmured in his heavy Czech accent.

I thought this was pretty ironic. Cersenka looked like shit. His health seemed to have deteriorated sharply in the two years since my own boss, Lenny Handelsman, and he had worked on that Broadway musical that had the misfortune of opening the night a major freak hurricane roared down the canyoned streets of New York City. The musical had been saved, but that largely was on the reputations of the show's director, Handelsman, and its dance master, Cersenka. Shortly after that run, Cersenka was rumored to have entered a private hospital, not to be heard from again until called forth for this momentous production.

Cersenka was still lithe and well-muscled and moved with a grace that was the hallmark of a premier dancer. But he was gaunt, his cheeks hollow, and his head had become bald and his scalp mottled with purple splotches since the last time I'd seen him. It was highly unlikely that Masters had missed the change in him in these two brief years.

"No, 'Mr. Masters' now, Milo," Masters said, with a jocular, almost genuine smile. "I'm so happy you have signed on with our little venture here."

"You call and I come," Cersenka answered.

"I could not have conceived of doing it without you," Masters answered.

I wondered if Cersenka could discern that Masters was full of shit on this point as well as I could. I handled all of Handelsman's correspondence. I knew that Masters had tried to engage someone else entirely for this production for months and had only reluctantly given in to Handelsman's begging that Cersenka be given the nod, that it was a production that he ached to do and that probably would be his last.

I thought on one of Masters' last letters to Handelsman on the subject in which he said he didn't want a dance master who would die in the middle of rehearsals. So I knew he knew that Cersenka wasn't well. And Handelsman knew that too.

I looked over at Handelsman to see his reaction, and he was smiling worshipfully at Masters, oblivious to the elder man's deceit. I registered an intent to punish the stage director for that when we'd gotten back to the yacht that night.

I'd heard that Masters, the playwright, and Handelsman, the stage director, had a close mentoring relationship some fifteen years earlier when the director was in his twenties and the playwright in his forties—that Masters had given Handelsman a leg up on Broadway by insisting that he be given productions of Masters' plays—and I knew Handelsman's proclivities—intimately—so perhaps something was becoming clear to me here. I took a moment to decide what that meant to me, whether I was jealous. But no I wasn't. My principal duty as Handelsman's "right-hand boy" might be to sleep with him and fuck him regularly. But I couldn't say that it bothered me that someone had been there before me. Not as long as Handelsman paid me well.

"So, what do we have here?" Masters, the playwright, asked as he leaned over the card table and looked at the pile of papers strewn around there.

"We didn't know what you planned," Lenny answered, so we have collected various configurations for the stage. "We're gathered now. Perhaps you can tell us—"

"You want to know what I have in my little case here that's worthy of the last production at Arena Stage before they close down for a total rebuild?" Masters asked. His eyes were twinkling; he was enjoying the grand tease.

Masters raised his arm and snapped his fingers without looking back behind him, and the young man who had followed him into the room, burdened down with cases and scrolls and unidentifiable lengths of material, materialized and pulled three bound manuscripts from a briefcase. Then, at Masters' sweeping direction, he bestowed one each on the stage director and the dance master, and gently, almost reverently, set the third one down on the table in front of where Masters was sitting. He then turned, set part of his burden down, pulled another folding chair up to a place about six feet behind Masters and to the side, and settled in the chair. He dug into the briefcase and extracted a fourth manuscript and perched it on his lap, pen in hand, ready to take notes.

Masters continued teasing the other two, admonishing them not to open the manuscripts yet, and giving them an interminable running story on the "intolerable" plane trip down to Washington, D.C., from New York. Handelsman's hands were trembling as he fingered the edges of the manuscript cover. Cersenka's face bore a somewhat pained look, as if a flash of heartburn was shooting through his chest.

I took these moments of tease to size up Masters' assistant, as I viewed the tableau at the card table from where I was standing in the shadows, not really in the group, leaning on the practice piano. He was small but well formed. Creamy milk-chocolate skin, but not Negroid. Some mix. Jamaican? Algerian? Curly black hair setting around his face like a halo; a face that was as much pretty as handsome. Broad, sensual, Bryonesque lips. Startling dark-chocolate brown eyes. I at first thought he was a teenager, but now that I looked at him more closely, I could see that he was just small of stature. And he had the grace in his movements of a dancer. I bet myself that's what he'd been when Masters took charge of him.

One thing was very clear. He worshipped Masters as much as the other two men at the table did.

11

He hung on every word Masters said, ever ready to be there, serving his every need, if summoned. And the gaze he trained on the back of Masters' head wasn't just one of subservience or respect. It was a look of love.

It seemed quite likely to me that Masters was fucking him—if I was right that Masters and Handelsman had such a relationship a decade and a half ago. If so, I envied Masters. The assistant looked quite fuckable to me too.

Masters' voice boomed out, signaling his change of topic, and I returned my attention to the card table tableau.

"You may open the manuscripts now," he said. He was so full of self-importance that I wished someone would take him down a notch. This was really Handelsman's show. When the five-decade-old Arena Stage, the acclaimed regional theater located at Washington, D.C.'s, southeast waterfront, decided to completely demolish its once-revolutionary theater complex, dominated by one of the nation's first theaters in the round, and totally rebuild, in a two-year process, it had wanted to go out with a bang. The theater was famous for discovering new acting and playwrighting talent and sending productions straight on to Broadway. For a last play in this complex, it wanted to extend that tradition in such a way that its reputation carried it through the dormant reconstruction years. And they had turned to Handelsman, a Broadway director at the height of his fame, to put together that production.

Bringing in Masters had been Handelsman's doing. Masters hadn't had a hit in several years, and, as much of an icon in the theater as he was, he probably wouldn't have quickly sprung to the minds of the ever-experimenting, edgy Arena Stage board for this particular play slot.

It would seem that Handelsman had picked well, though, because even as he and Cersenka were turning the cover board of the manuscript, I heard them gasp in harmony—and it was a gasp of appreciative delight.

"Can this be?" Handelsman exclaimed.

"I said there would be seven," Masters said. "I know it's been a decade, but this is my proposal for the production."

"I don't know what to say," Handelsman said. "You could take this directly to Broadway. Any producer and any theater on Broadway would clear time and space for this. You would have no trouble finding financial backing, on the strength of the concept alone, even in these tight times."

"I believe the occasion is worthy of it," Masters said in that supercilious voice, which, however had the clear ring of authority and entitlement to it.

"Another of the 'D' plays? A new play? I was expecting a revival of one of your many Broadway triumphs. But another 'D' play? We will eclipse Broadway for its run."

"That is the idea, yes," Masters said. "And not just another 'D' play—the last 'D' play. Its premier. Here in Washington . . . at Arena Stage. I do believe they will remember that for two years at least, if I do say so myself."

I couldn't fault Masters on that statement, as egotistical as it was. He had won three Pulitzers and five Tonys for five of the earlier 'D' plays, called these because of the alliteration of their titles, which thus far had progressed from *Delight,* to *Desire,* to *Decadence,* to *Deceit,* and then to *Descent.* Only the last, *Descent,* had not lived up to the legend in its Broadway run. And there were those who doubted then that there ever would be the seventh 'D' play that Masters had boasted of. After that, Masters had a spate of misses, plays that were good but not memorable, that didn't match the quality and impact of the first five 'D' plays. There was talk than that he had lost his edge—and even after his last two plays, which had returned to the brilliance of his early work, he was being talked about in theater circles in the past tense—which had made Handelsman's insistence of a Masters play for this venue all the more curious and risky.

But it seems that Handelsman's trust had been well founded. And I found myself racking my brain, trying to figure out what this seventh and last play in the series was titled.

"*Defiance*?" Cersenka questioned, speaking up for the first time since they had opened the manuscript and thus answering the question that had been in my mind. How strange. Not an ending really, but seemingly more the beginning of a new cycle.

"Precisely," Masters said, his voice warm with triumph, proud of his work and of the surprise it engendered. "The unexpected. I always intended the unexpected at this point. I know what everyone was thinking, what they were thinking the final title would be . . ."

"*Death*," Cersenka whispered in a ghostly voice, stopping everyone in the room in their tracks, causing them to hold their breath, the heavy silence punctuated by the hacking cough Cersenka devolved to after interjecting that word into the air.

After a minute, Masters sniffed and said, "Yes, well. I know what people thought. But I always thought that would be a bit too obvious."

"Obvious, yes," Cersenka said. "But it's there, isn't it? It's there in all of them, all of the 'D' plays, lurking in the background, pointing to it, leading up to it. Death."

Masters looked radiant, accepting what Cersenka was saying as an accolade to his talent. But then he said enigmatically. "Perhaps yes, perhaps no. You have not read this last script."

"Yes, well, perhaps it is time that I did," Cersenka said. "We have not that much time to stage an entirely new production. I too assumed it would be a revival. Something that could be slightly reshaped, brought into the current decade. But a whole new play . . ."

He paused momentarily to let the task that was before them sink in; they were all stage professionals of the first rank. They all knew a new production for the Arena Stage, given the time frame, would be a Herculean task. But all three, including Cersenka, had been infused with excitement from the moment they realized that they quite possibly had an earth-shattering event in their grasp.

"It has dancing scenes, this last play?" Cersenka then asked, obviously not yet fully believing. "And a score? It already has a score?"

"Yes, of course," Masters answered in a slightly wounded voice. "That has been key through the series. They all have dance sequences. And, yes, certainly it

15

has a score—but you will be able to recognize themes in the score from the earlier six plays. That is purposeful. This is the last, the linking play. The glue to my masterpiece."

"Then I best get started," Cersenka said. "If you gentlemen will excuse me. I have a score to review and dancers to hire." He rose, apparently in some pain, took up an ivory-headed cane, and started to move toward the double doors at the other end of the shadowed room. He stopped, though, beside the chair of Masters' assistant and took the surprised young man's chin in his hand and lifted his face.

"You are a dancer, are you not?" I was amazed that Cersenka had reached the same conclusion as I had about the young man. I had not noticed that he had realized the youth was in the room at all.

The beautiful young man cleared his throat in embarrassment at the attention paid him, and answered in a small, melodic voice. "I was, yes . . . I was. But not now. Now I work for Mr. Masters."

"Perhaps, though. Just perhaps you still want to dance," Cersenka said. "Yes, I see it in your face. Perhaps, just perhaps I will see you at the auditions."

Even more embarrassed now, the young man moved his chin from Cersenka's gentle grip, and his eyes returned to the back of his boss—I could just as easily say "of his master."

"I don't think—"
"Well, perhaps," Cersenka repeated, and then he turned and tapped his way, slowly, yet gracefully straight for the exit.

Neither Masters nor Handelsman had seemed to notice this exchange at all, they were already so deeply

16

engrossed in preliminary discussions about the coming production. But I certainly noticed. Handelsman had worked with Cersenka before. I had been there. I knew Cersenka. He would not have a single dancer in his troupe for a production that he did not fully control, fully possess. He fucked them all; that was the symbol, the acknowledgment of the control he had over them, individually and as a troupe. The sexual dynamics in the room had just been kicked up a notch—and the Master apparently hadn't even noticed it.

My attention was arrested by the scraping of chairs. Masters and Handelsman were rising from the table, and Handelsman was scooping together the papers strewn on the table top and motioning me to come over and help him. Masters snapped his fingers as well, and the young assistant dutifully stood up and started to take up the gear he'd brought into the room, most of which Masters had made no use of.

"I have invited Creigh and his assistant to the yacht, where we can discuss this more comfortably and over drinks and dinner. Show his assistant to the ship, will you, Gil? Creigh and I will be along shortly, after we have broken this momentous news to the theater director."

"Sure thing, Lenny," I answered. Masters may have his assistant cowed, but I was the top in the relationship between me and my employer. He was the one who opened his legs to me and begged for the fuck, who moaned at the working of my cock inside him. We were well beyond the Mr. Handelsman stage, Lenny and I.

As I approached the young man, his eyes went big, as if he'd seen me for the first time. And perhaps he was seeing me for the first time. I would pretty much have blended with the shadows where I was standing over at the side by the practice piano. And he had only had eyes for his employer.

And I could well understand how he would be taken aback when he first saw me. I was at least a foot taller than he was and, from his perception, a hulking—maybe even a menacing—presence.

He turned away from me to gather up the rest of the paraphernalia he had brought into the room, and I felt an intake of breath and my cock started to swell. He had a beautiful butt. Nicely rounded butt cheeks and trousers tailored to show his crack. The close-fitting legs of the trousers revealed strong, well-muscled thighs. I had obviously been right. A dancer, and a well-exercised one too. He must still practice. I wondered if Masters knew he was still practicing, or whether this was the young man's secret, the last vestige of a grab for independence. I didn't think Masters would be pleased to know that the young man hadn't completely given up his dream for him.

As we turned to walk out of the room, I laid a hand on the small of his back, ostensibly to guide him in the right direction toward where the yacht was moored not more than a hundred yards from the theater complex, at the Capitol Yacht Club on the Washington Channel, a finger off the Potomac River, at Water Street. This had been one of Handelsman's stipulations to taking on this production; he required mooring rights within a short walk of the theater so that he could continue to live in the style—and isolation—that he had become accustomed to.

My hand was like that of a giant compared to the young man's diminutive size. I felt him shudder when I laid my palm on him, but I also heard him give a little sigh. And I caught him looking up into my face— although I don't think he knew I saw his expression. I knew he was impressed by the size of me. If he only knew. He would certainly tremble if he could see the size of my cock.

And there, right then, I became determined that he *would* see the size of my cock. I decided that I would have him sometime during our shared stay here. The rehearsal and production time for this play would take a minimum of three months, maybe even four if the play did so well that they put off the start of demolition, which I knew was covered as a possibility in Handelsman's contract. I'd never required more than a week to have any man I wanted.

As we moved into the darkness of the corridor outside the dance rehearsal room, we had to turn to the right and go down a flight of unlit stairs to get to an exit out onto 6th Street. In redirecting the young man, I let my hand move down and cup one of his butt cheeks. I felt him tremble, but he said nothing and didn't attempt to shake away from my hand.

I laughed when we reached the street, and I pointed to where a walkway would give us access to Water Street across the wider and busier Maine Avenue. He asked me why I laughed, but I dared not tell him the truth.

I had laughed at the image of the dance master, Miloslav Cersenka, and me in a race to cuckold the great, cocky Creighton Masters.

Chapter Two: Sean

I could tell that Mr. Masters was nervous about this first meeting with the director and dance master at Arena Stage that afternoon. He had been peevish and snappish all morning—well, more so than usual—finding fault with everything and being detailed about the clothes he wanted me to lay out for the meeting and then rejecting them and upbraiding me for what I thought went together and was appropriate. And mostly I knew he was on edge because he had accosted me on the upstairs landing, taken me down to ground like a lion pouncing on a gazelle, stripped my trousers off, and fucked me hard and cruelly, giving no heed to whether or not I was comfortable, and not noticing—or caring—that my head was bouncing off the stair railings.

But this was not new to me. Mr. Masters was always like this before an important performance. Nervous, overcompensating for his unacknowledged flashes of self-doubt, and randy. I could smell the sex on him—his precum and musky "marking" scent, the building of lust—as he built up to preperformance nerves. I knew it was coming, and I knew that when he grabbed me wherever I was, I was to open my legs to him as I tumbled to the ground or the table top or over the chair arm or on the bed, to relax and open myself to his thick master's tool as he plowed up into me in one killing thrust—like a lion. And a lion he was, and there was many a young man in the theater who envied me for having Mr. Masters' cock stretching and punishing my channel. He was a lion of the theater, a Pulitzer-winning playwright. A great talent. Still. Or at least there still were those who granted him that status. I celebrate that status and being permitted to live in his shadow. I wouldn't say I granted him anything. He took whatever he wanted from me.

I could understand why Mr. Masters was nervous today. We had nothing else coming up on the schedule other than this special production at Arena Stage in Washington, D.C., to mark the venerable, highly acclaimed regional theater's closing for two years for a total rebuild of facilities. The theater had contracted a first-rate New York director, Leonard Handelsman, to stage a high-profile closer play, and Handelsman, over some opposition, had insisted that my employer, Creighton Masters, pick one of his own plays for that production.

Mr. Masters had the necessary name value, but he was considered past his peak. And he was taking a risk in what he was going to propose today, because Handelsman no doubt was expecting a revival of one of Mr. Master's highly successful early career plays. But Mr. Masters was going to propose a new play—and although his last two had done well with the critics and the box offices, he had a spate of "not quites" before that and since the staging of the fifth of his acclaimed "D" plays. The sixth of the "D" plays, *Descent,* had been the first of his "not quite" nonsuccesses.

I ascribed his "down" period to the auto accident that killed his former assistant and live-in lover, Lawrence. It took several years for Mr. Masters to recover from that loss—only surmounted when he took me on in the role Lawrence once had fulfilled.

What he was going to suggest—no, demand—today was the staging of the seventh and last of these plays—he had always said there would be seven, and when asked by the press "why seven?" he'd always shot off a flippant, "there were seven deadly sins."

But after the nonsuccess of the sixth "D" play, no one ever expected this series to be completed.

Defiance was his seventh play, and, as I knew and no one else did, he hadn't done much of the work on it at all—in fact, he hadn't written more than barebones outlines for years. The well seemed to be dry. Both he and I were counting on a success with *Defiance* to start his creative juices again. So, there was every reason for him to be nervous about selling himself at this meeting; we were near the end of the road.

No one but me knew how long we'd been near the end of that road. The polishing of those last two stage successes and even the bulk of *Defiance* were my writing, not his. He still had the spark of genius. He still knew the hooks that grabbed the theatergoer and inspired the actor to deliver his or her best work. But he could do no more than paint with a broad brush now. I had been filling in the detail work.

Still, it was his genius and in honor of his early brilliance that brought me to him and that kept me with him despite his extraordinary demands on my life, not the least the sexual demands. But that's what you do for a lion of the theater. You live in his shadow and do all you can to keep his armor burnished. And I lived in hope—in the hope that he would regain his greatness for the detail work as well as the brilliant broad brush.

We weren't broke, but, given Mr. Masters' lavish lifestyle, we perpetually were close to that. Everything about the man was bigger than life—not just his physical presence and his charisma and robust body and good looks, which he had maintained into his late fifties, but his living and spending as well. He was a legend in the theater and had knowledge of that and every expectation of living up to it.

A case in point was this townhouse on 7th Street in Southeast Washington within a short walking distance of Arena Stage on the Washington Channel waterfront. When Mr. Masters heard that Leonard Handelsman, the director, had brought his quite large yacht in and docked it right on the waterfront near the theater in the Capitol Yacht Club, Mr. Masters had been determined we weren't going to be upstaged and insisted on renting this small townhouse—just a wedge of a two-story place in fifties' style modern. Mostly glass, with a living, dining, and kitchen combination downstairs and a loft bedroom above. All for an astronomical price even by New York standards.

But I had to admit that it would be convenient to the stage, if Mr. Masters was able to sell his idea of risking it all on the concluding play of the "D" series. If.

I worried a bit about Handelsman. He could have gotten any playwright he wanted for this production. It was guaranteed to be highlighted in theater circles this coming season. Why had he chosen Mr. Masters? They weren't contemporaries. Mr. Masters was a good fifteen years older than Handelsman, and Handelsman was at the height of his theater world presence. He was in the theater stratosphere and still climbing. Mr. Masters was on the descent, and the question of whether he was still in the stratosphere was moot—and even more a question to me, who knew our true position.

But there seemed to be some advantage Mr. Masters had with Handelsman.

As we entered the dance practice room in the Arena Stage complex, where the all-important initial planning meeting was to take place, I saw at once that there was more to the Masters-Handelsman connection than I had supposed. Handelsman was reacting toward Mr. Masters as if he was a visiting god—which, of course, encouraged Mr. Masters to act even more the part. I could sense his reassurance building. And that would mean more sex after the meeting. Mr. Masters celebrated his ups as vigorously as he compensated for his nerves. Mr. Masters was still vigorous and oversexed for his stage of life—and he was built for it.

I couldn't help but turn my attention to the third person at the flimsy card table in the middle of the vast, dimly lit, polished-floor dance studio as I settled in a folding chair a good six feet behind Mr. Masters and just out of the periphery of his vision. Placed just so, I could "hop to" to meet his frequent demands for documents and scripts from the overwhelming collection of items he had insisted I manhandle over to the meeting—most of them purely for show and bravado.

I was in my element here. A dance studio. And the third man sitting at the table was the dean of Broadway dancing, a legend in his own right, Miloslav Cersenka. I was actually a little taken aback at seeing him. Rumors were floating around Broadway that he was dead. And, indeed, he hadn't worked a show there in two years. And yet here he was, in the flesh, although the flesh these days was weak. He was still powerfully built, but his body was gaunt and almost cadaverous, only his dedication to dance seeming to enable him to hold on to muscle tone. His skin was translucent, and there were blotches of bruising on his arms and on one cheek and on his bald, cadaverous scalp. More damning—for him, at least—there was an ivory-headed cane propped up against the table by his side. If some leg ailment prevented him from dancing, he might as well be dead. Not dead perhaps. Not yet. But not far.

I had once worshipped Miloslav Cersenka. It was he who brought me to New York from my Midwestern town. Not he himself, physically, but the legend of him. I was a dancer. Tatesville, Ohio, was no place for a young man to be a dancer. Tatesville, Ohio, was a bedrock of high school football. I was built slight and said to be "too pretty" to try to make it on the football field, especially as dark-skinned players were supposed to be big bruisers with dreadlocks on the line. I had been drawn early into the world of dance instead. That was no talent to have in Tatesville. It flagged you as a pansy. And sure enough, shortly after my eighteenth birthday, the vice principal of the school trapped me backstage in the high school auditorium late one afternoon, and when I went home that night I no longer was a virgin.

The problem was that I enjoyed it.

And that, coupled with my love for dance, meant I had to leave Tatesville. I saw movie musicals at the local theater, and I noted that, more often than not,

Miloslav Cersenka was credited as the dance arranger and director. I read up on everything I could find on Cersenka, and then, when the opportunity came, I went to New York to break into the theater, hopefully in one of Cersenka's productions.

As I auditioned, never reaching the heights of a Cersenka production, I heard that you had to devote yourself totally to Cersenka to be one of his production dancers. Totally. It was said that he insisted on fucking all of his dancers, male and female, and that only through this level of control would he trust a dancer to work in his troupe, to surrender all to him and to deliver exactly what he commanded.

That was no problem for me, but I'd never managed to land an audition with Cersenka himself.

Before that ever happened, I landed an audition with Creighton Masters. An audition of a similar kind, but without the hope of dancing at the end.

I was dancing in the off-Broadway launch of one of Mr. Masters' "not quite" plays three years previously, a play that didn't get to Broadway and didn't make much of a splash off Broadway either. I was glad to get the work, but I knew my dancing wasn't getting me where I wanted to go.

I was vulnerable. Creighton Masters was a big deal to me. And he was such a sad figure then, always looking almost lost through prolonged mourning of his assistant and lover, Lawrence. When he suggested we lunch together one afternoon, several hours before the show, I was thrilled.

I assumed we would be in a group, but we weren't. He turned all of his charm on me—just me. I doubt anyone but those who have come under Mr.

Masters' spell would understand how flattering and disarming that was. He asked me if I wanted to see his suite. Then he had wine delivered and told me to amuse myself—that he felt like taking a bath. Then he asked me to come in and scrub his back. Then he asked me to undress and join him in the tub. And I said yes to it all. Without a second thought. This was Creighton Masters, the lion of playwrights. He was on his back in the tub and pulled me down onto his lap, facing him, and embraced my chest tightly in his arms and thrust up into me with a cock I never could imagine that he had. And while I moaned and groaned at the taking—a possession more filling and vigorous and deep than I had ever known before—he marked me as his. As he fucked me a second time that afternoon, he offered me the position as his assistant.

I danced that night, in pain, and my legs not able to close. But that was my last appearance on stage.

I had been practicing the last several months, preparing for a return, if our financial circumstance dictated that would be necessary. Not knowing if I could ever again be even as good as I was when I stopped. But knowing we needed contingencies. I, of course, hadn't let Mr. Masters know this. He would have been outraged. He would have considered it treasonous, I knew, at the thought that I doubted in the least that he could continue as he always had.

It was this thought of maybe returning, however, that made me melt at being in the same room with Miloslav Cersenka, not more than ten feet from where he was sitting. I had never hoped to be this close to the dance master.

I handed out scripts at Mr. Masters' direction, and he asked the other two not to open the covers initially. He was waiting for his moment, this man of high theatrical drama. And in the interlude, I had been reminiscing—on how Mr. Masters had come into my life—rather how I had come into his—and how drastically my life had changed at that point. My attention went back to the men at the table when I heard Handelsman and Cersenka gasp. Mr. Masters had let them open the covers and see the title—*Defiance*.

"Can this be?" Handelsman was exclaiming.

"I said there would be seven," Masters answered. "I know it's been a decade, but this is my proposal for the production."

"I don't know what to say," Handelsman said. "You could take this directly to Broadway. Any producer and any theater on Broadway would clear time and space for this. You would have no trouble finding financial backing, on the strength of the concept alone, even in these tight times."

"I believe the occasion is worthy of it," Masters answered in that dismissive voice I knew so well. I knew even more about that voice, though. I knew it was the product of desperation.

"Another of the 'D' plays? A new play? I expected a revival of one of your many Broadway triumphs. But another 'D' play? We will eclipse Broadway for its run."

"That is the idea, yes," Masters said. "And not just another 'D' play—the last 'D' play. Its premier. Here in Washington . . . at Arena Stage. I do believe they will remember that for two years at least, if I do say so myself."

It was then that I discerned another presence in the room. It must have been some movement in the shadows over by the practice piano that had arrested my attention. I looked over there, but it was just too murky. But, yes, there did seem to be another man, a tall, dark man, leaning on the top of the piano at the far side of it from here. I wondered why I couldn't see him better.

I heard the name of the seventh "D" play, and my attention went back to the animated discussion between Mr. Masters and Handelsman and the dance master.

"*Defiance?*" Cersenka was saying, a question mark in his voice.

"Precisely," Masters said in a voice that told me he thought he had won them over now. "The unexpected. I always intended the unexpected at this point. I know what everyone was thinking, what they were thinking the final title would be—"

"*Death,*" Cersenka whispered in a hollow, faraway voice. And then everyone stopped whatever they were doing, as Cersenka was coughing a deep-throated cough. Bringing something into the room that hadn't been there before. A sense of reality? Of inevitability?

After a minute, Masters sniffed and said, "Yes, well. I know what people thought. But I always thought that would be a bit too obvious."

"Obvious, yes," Cersenka said. "But it's there, isn't it? It's there in all of them, all of the 'D' plays, lurking in the background. Death."

I knew then that Mr. Masters was in his element. They had been won over. They were looking deeply in the play, taking it seriously. Our play. Well, now, I couldn't think that—not "our" play; I was being presumptuous. My contribution couldn't have been significant—and it certainly couldn't be voiced. Mr. Masters' play. His concluding masterpiece of the "D" series. He looked Cersenka directly in the eye then and said, "Perhaps yes, perhaps no. You have not read this last script."

It wasn't long before Cersenka had made his exit of the room, leaning on his cane in a heartbreaking, slow progression to the door, and stopping beside me and embarrassing and pleasing me deeply by guessing correctly that I was a dancer and by offering me an audition for the play. And then the other two men at the table, oblivious to how momentous it was to me to receive that attention from Cersenka, were rising, scraping their chairs on the polished wood floor. The stage director, Handelsman, scooped together the papers strewn on the table top, and I saw him motioning toward the piano in the shadows.

My breath stopped and I gasped inwardly as a black giant emerged from the shadows. No wonder I hadn't been able to see who was lurking back there. He was ebony black and was wearing a black turtleneck and black trousers. He was a hulking muscle man, but he moved gracefully on the balls of his feet as he came over to the table at Handelsman's summons. He was a handsome man. He could have played a tribal African chief on stage. And all eyes would have gone to him whenever he was there. I wondered if he was a dancer or an actor.

But then Mr. Masters snapped his fingers at me, and I started gathering up all of that gear he had made me bring over for appearances sake, pushing my selfish dreams of dancing for Cersenka into the back of my brain.

Handelsman was speaking to the black giant, who was being attentive to him, although I felt by his bearing that the black man saw himself as in no way subservient to the stage director. "I have invited Creigh and his assistant to the yacht, where we can discuss this more comfortably and over drinks and dinner," Handelsman said. "Show his assistant to the ship, will you, Gil? Creigh and I will be along shortly, after we have broken this momentous news to the theater director."

"Sure thing, Lenny," the black man answered in a breezy tone, which I then got the impression he was using to impress me—to show me the difference between me as Mr. Masters' dogs body and him—because he introduced himself to me as Gil Johnson, Leonard Handelsman's assistant.

Johnson was giving me "that" look—as if he could see straight through me and the relationship I had with Mr. Masters, as if he knew I was nothing better than a sex slave to Mr. Masters. And, disconcertingly, as if he, the big black man, already owned me as well.

I turned away from him in embarrassment and not wanting to let him see that I was impressed by him, that something at the center of me was showing interest in him. I gathered up the rest of the paraphernalia I'd brought into the room. When I was upright again, he pointed to the doors at the back of the room.

As we turned to walk out of the room, he laid a hand on the small of my back to guide me in the right direction, which I enjoyed. Then, outside the room, when we turned right to go down a dark flight of stairs that led to an exit out on 6th Street, the black giant moved his hand down to cup my buttocks. Just like he knew he'd made me already.

Out on the street, he turned to me and smiled. "They won't need us. We can go to the yacht later rather than sooner. You've got the keys to this townhouse of Masters', don't you?" He squeezed my butt cheek in his broad hand and was leaning in close to me. I liked the feel of his hand. It burned right into my ass. But I wasn't free to do what I wanted. Masters demanded exclusivity. He never wanted to wear a condom; he said he did everything on the spur of the moment and condoms disrupted the moment. I wasn't free to fuck anyone else—no matter how inviting this obvious offer was.

"Mr. Masters will expect me to be there when he arrives," I said.

"This Mr. Masters owns you, I take it?" the black giant asked. But he was still smiling and seemed to be amused.

"Pretty much so, yes," I answered. There could be no meeting, no relationship. So there was no reason for me to be coy.

"OK, I'll take you on over to the yacht. But I don't think I'll stay around very long. And I don't think you will either."

I wondered what he meant by that as we walked the two blocks over to the waterfront, but then, when I saw the yacht, I was mesmerized. It was one of those old fantail yachts from the 1920s, all polished teak superstructure on top of a glistening white hull. Pretty long, but small enough to get into a channel like this. I figured it made a pretty nifty home away from home, though.

Gil Johnson waited with me, asking me about my background and being guarded about his in return, until Mr. Masters and Handelsman arrived, all animated talk. Once embarked, they walked right by us where we were sitting in the semicircle of cushions at the stern of the ship, entered the salon, and disappeared down a corridor at the far end of that toward the bow of the ship.

"Have a nice wait," Gil said, with a smirk on his face, as he rose from the cushions. "When you get tired enough to want to go home, go take a look. I'm outta here until nine. If you want to stay around until I'm back and then want to go do something, the offer's still open."

I thanked him through pursed lips and then watched him saunter off up the dock and onto Water Street and over toward the bars near the Gangplank restaurant. He looked mighty fine from the back, moving like he was totally confident, in self-assured strides. I regretted more than somewhat my pledge of constancy to Mr. Masters. I well knew there weren't many black people in the theater, but, with this man's presence, he could rule the stage.

I sat there for the better part of an hour, on the fantail of the yacht, *Boxoffice*. I'm sure many thought that was a funny name for a ship. But it made sense for Leonard Handelsman. He'd probably paid for it from the big box-office returns of his plays on Broadway.

Then I started thinking about Mr. Masters and Handelsman. Handelsman had been so deferential back there in the meeting room at the Arena Stage, and the longer Mr. Masters had been there, the more self-assured he'd become. There was about a decade and a half between them; I couldn't imagine when they would have met. Then I noticed an album out on a table near the door into the salon. It was open, as if someone had been reviewing it out here. It wouldn't be something you'd leave out on the deck of a ship, with all of the salt-water breezes around, even though this area was covered. I got up and picked up the book, and brought it back to the bench seat, and started to scan through the pages.

It was a scrapbook history of Handelsman's Broadway productions. And there, in the first few pages, where Handelsman started his rise to acclaim, there were playbills and photos that answered my question. Handelsman's start was at the height of Mr. Masters' stage hits. The playbills and photos alike explained it. Mr. Masters had given Handelsman a leg up. So, it stood to reason that Handelsman was giving payback now. Just what a young, rising star would do for his mentor. But the photos were a bit more disturbing. They were group photos, but there, always, were Mr. Masters and Handelsman together, touching—intimately so. Nothing for sure, of course, if you didn't know Mr. Masters intimately yourself. I recognized those expressions, the possessiveness of the way Mr. Masters held his arm around the young Handelsman's shoulders, the way he put his hand on Handelsman's forearm.

So, I wasn't that surprised when I heard the faint, but not unfamiliar sounds wafting up the corridor leading toward the bow on the other side of the salon.

Slowly, silently, not really wanting to do it, I entered the salon and started working my way down that corridor. Immediately after the salon, there were staterooms on either side. Two on the left. Just one at that depth on the right. No doubt the owner's stateroom. The sounds were more distinct now. They were coming from the open door beyond the stateroom on the right.

It was a small cabin. Not much more room available than for the sling suspended from an iron hook in the center of the ceiling. Handelsman was in the sling, his head pointed away from me, toward the outside wall, his legs trussed up in hoops high on the chains nearer to the door that attached the black leather sling to the hook in the ceiling. He was naked—and in great shape for a man in his forties. The soles of his feet were moving back and forth, his head was lolled over the far end of the sling, and he was moaning deeply—the way I'm sure I moaned when Mr. Masters was fucking me.

Mr. Masters was standing, between Handelsman's spread and trussed legs. The sight was as mesmerizing as it was horrifying to me. There was a good rhythm going to it. I could see Mr. Masters' butt cheeks expand and contract in rhythm to the movement of Handelsman's feet. And with each contraction of Mr. Masters' butt cheeks, representing the slide of his cock deep inside Handelsman's channel, Handelsman emitted a moan.

I turned and retraced my steps, walking smartly, but silently. And I didn't stop when I got to the fantail. I moved on to the gangplank and crossed it and walked across the concrete apron on the quay and up a little grassy rise to where there were park benches, set inside the sidewalk on Water Street, pointed toward the yacht basin.

There were few others around, it having gotten a little nippy out as night had fallen. The lights in the rigging of the boats tied to the piers and the view beyond to the Haines Point park, separating the channel from the Potomac River, and the lights of the runways of Reagan Airport across the river should have been cheering. But I wasn't in a cheerful mood, and the lights were bleary as they reflected off the tears welling up in my eyes.

It wasn't just the betrayal. A man of Mr. Masters' importance and standing doesn't betray. He just lives, and everyone around him adjusts. And it wasn't the hypocrisy of demanding constancy from me and not exercising it himself or even the horror of what it could mean when he had unprotected sex with me and was fucking other men. It was more because of my weakness, because of my own irrational connection to him. I wasn't blinded by Mr. Masters' self-centeredness or some of the realities behind his "great man" façade. In fact, I loved him all the more for it. He was one of the great men of the theater—and he had let me into the center of his life.

I realized it was jealousy I felt. The obvious prior relationship with Handelsman. The swift and easy way they just drifted matter-of-factly back into a sexual relationship. Leaving me to cool my heels on the fan tail of that son of a bitch's yacht. I felt so, so small.

"You OK?"

I turned and looked up. It was the black giant, Gil whateverhisnamewas. Gil Johnson, I guess. He plopped down beside me and turned to me.

"What are you doing up here? Isn't it warmer down on the ship?"

"I . . . I couldn't." I was having trouble saying anything.

"They're fucking, aren't they?" He asked, obviously not the least bit surprised. "They just walked on by you and went in to Lenny's special room and started fucking, didn't they?"

"Yes." I tried not to make my answer sound desperate. But there was no way I brought that off.

"You didn't know, did you?" He continued. "You didn't know anything about Masters and Handelsman's shared history before you came down to Washington, did you?"

"No," I squeaked. He put his arm around me then. And I let him. He was warm. And he smelled nice. I could feel the strength in his arms. And apparently something about that conveyed to him, because his next question was directly related.

"Hey. Firm shoulders and biceps. And I saw you move back in the meeting room. Dancer are you?"

"Yes, yes I am . . . or was," I said.

"Masters make you give it up?"

I didn't answer, which gave him the answer. Instead, I tried to redirect. "You move like a dancer too. You a dancer too?"

He laughed. "No, I'm a kick boxer. Reaches a similar result, but that's a whole other bag, I can assure you."

He was putting me in my place. Just like they did back in Tatesville. Separating the athletes from the pansies. But I'd come a long way since then. I just let it roll over me.

"But you work for Handelsman," I said. Trying to get a little of my own back.

"Yeah, he gives me my paycheck. But it's not a bit like you workin' for Masters, I can assure you of that too."

Masters was fucking Handelsman. So this big black guy was fucking Handelsman too. I was feeling weak in the knees. My body wanted him. And Mr. Masters had thrown me a curve.

He might have had me nailed right then and there, but he veered off the subject.

"You dancin' in this production?"

"No," I said. "I haven't danced in a production for a few years."

"Since you started workin' for Masters then?"

I didn't answer. Which, again, was an answer.

"You're hard bodied, though," at which he took the opportunity to give me a good feel here and there, "so you've been practicin'."

"Just recently," I answered. "I . . . I'm thinking of going back to it—to dancing on the stage."

"Does Masters know?"

"No." I said it softly, but he heard me.

"Do you think he'll let you go back into it?"

"I don't know."

He turned my face toward his then, and he put his lips to mine. I let him do that, but he became more aggressive and moved to slipping his tongue in past my lips. I broke away from the kiss and turned my head to where I was looking away from him, up the channel, toward where it joined with the mouth of the Anacostia River into the wider Potomac. While he was kissing me, he'd placed one of his big paws on my basket. I didn't have to tell him that I found him attractive.

"He fucks you, doesn't he?" Gil asked softly.

"Yes," I answered. But my face was pointed away from him and the answer was caught in the wind.

"What was that?"

"Yes," I said louder and I turned back to him. I'm sure he could see the tears in my eyes.

"Whenever he wants, right?"

"Yes," I answered. But I couldn't leave it like that. "He's Creighton Masters. He's a lion of the theater."

"Big cock has he?" Gil asked. He was smiling a sloppy grin. I should have taken that as mocking, but the way he said it encouraged me not to. It was like he was chipping at ice here, trying to get me.

"No . . . yes." I was flustered. "I meant that he is a legend in the theater, and my whole life is the theater. He's big and I'm small. Insignificant. And without him, I'd be even more insignificant. But yes . . . yes, he's got a cock to match his fame."

The smile stayed in place. "I got a big cock too. A legendary cock. I'd like to fuck you."

That moment had passed. He'd had me there for a few seconds. But that was way back in the conversation. Maybe it was because he was being so cocky, so sure of himself—although, god knows, how I was reacting to his paw cupping my cock and balls gave him every reason to be sure of himself. Being cocky and sure of himself, and I'd just been brought to the brink of that cockiness by Mr. Masters back there in Handelsman's "special" cabin.

I pulled away and stood up from the bench. But my legs weren't in on the program. They didn't carry me right away. Maybe I thought Gil required some sort of explanation. Because in other circumstances . . .

"I can't. Sorry, I can't. Mr. Masters requires exclusivity."

Gil laughed. Obviously my attempt at an explanation had hit his funny bone.

"Your Mr. Masters is back there banging the wadding out of my Mr. Handelsman, and you're worried about him demanding that you be exclusively his?"

"I don't expect you to understand," I said. I was feeling better now. The spell was broken. I was passed whatever I was being tempted to do.

"What's to understand?" Gil asked in an incredulous tone.

"Mr. Masters is Mr. Masters, and I am me. It nice that you have a different arrangement with Handelsman, but that's between you and him. Now, could you just go on back to the boat? That's where you sleep, isn't it?"

"Yes," he said. "I sleep wherever I want on the boat. But I usually sleep in the master's cabin with my dick up Handelsman's ass. So, who do you think that makes the master?"

"Who signs the checks?" I asked.

He stood up now too, and I could see that what I'd said had gotten to him. But he didn't strike out. He just started walking off in that sexy lope of his, down the grassy embankment, toward the *Boxoffice*.

At the bottom of the incline, he turned and looked up at me. He was standing between streetlights, a dark man in the shadows. I couldn't tell what expression was on his face.

"After what you've seen, you're going to sit there, waiting for Masters? In the chilly air?"

"Yes," I answered.

"Why?"

"Because he told me to."

I heard a harsh laugh, and he turned and took a step, but then stopped and turned again.

"That's a difference. Even if Lenny tells me to wait, I don't if I don't want to. But I'll tell you something else. I'm willing to wait for you. Just don't take too long."

And then he was gone, walking up the gangplank of Handelsman's yacht.

I felt relieved when Gil was back aboard the *Boxoffice*. It was a crazy night. I don't know what I would have done if he'd walked back up the grassy embankment and told me to follow him—that we were going to fuck.

Chapter Three: Gil

The little fucker had turned me down. I knew there wasn't anything ultimate or final about it, but I also knew he wanted me. What a tease, I thought, as I walked down the gangplank of the *Boxoffice* and started along the edge of the water on the path leading to the yacht harbors restaurant area to get something to eat and then maybe take a stroll toward the city to add to the old nest egg fund. He intrigued me. Not many black male dancers made it to Broadway; those who did tended to be eye catching. This dude certainly was eye catching.

Adding to the escape fund was what I'd programmed for this evening. It's just that Sean Singleton, Masters' assistant, was such a nice little piece, I thought I'd just do it for pleasure for a change. But he turned me down. Didn't make me want him any less, though.

So off I went to do a little work for myself rather than Handelsman. I wasn't too happy with Lenny at the moment. I didn't like the way he looked at that Masters guy. I didn't have enough escape money shuffled together yet for him to be looking at the Masters guy like that and not locked into me.

After taking care of the hunger pangs, I walked the six blocks up toward the Capitol building. But not all the way there; just to the edge of the Southwest Freeway, where, in the shadow of that elevated faster route out of town, I saw the signs for the Bachelor Pad.

I'd been told about this place when we were still up in New York. I had friends back there who knew I was trying to work my way from here to someplace else, and they told me the Bachelor Pad was a good place to pick up some quick major cash. It was on the edge of the gay section, such as it was, but close enough to the Capitol building and all of the congressional offices and a few major federal departments to attract men of power and money.

The place didn't seem to know what it wanted to be. I walked in and I had two choices—well, maybe three. In addition to rooms on either side of the hall, there was a staircase in the hall going up as well. As far as I knew, they had something going on up there too. To my right was a plush bar area. Very high tone; wouldn't be out of place in a Manhattan hotel. And to the left was a smoke-filled pool hall. The characters of the evening had parted themselves off by natural selection. Three-piece suits and Martini glasses in the bar. This contrasted with T-shirts with cigarette packs rolled up in sleeves and dirty long hair in the pool hall. I had my choice of soft elevator music and muted, intense conversations or the beat of a nervous drum and raucous cussing and intense crotch grabbing.

I wanted an extra paycheck and someone at risk enough to get what he wanted and evaporate into the night, not a break of the balls with down-home boys who'd want to rock the night away. So I turned to the right.

I was underdressed, but what I lacked in that, I made up for in stage presence. That's something I learned from Handelsman—how to enter a room and own it from the first step inside. Within seconds, nobody noticed I was just a hulking, out-of-place black guy in a black turtleneck and trousers. I was suddenly the most interesting—the most wanted—guy in the room—at least by the gaggle of bottoms gathered in the corner, ogling the more macho guys, and twittering among themselves. I sauntered over to the bar and ordered a beer.

"No, the bottle will be fine," I said. Part of owning the room is making it move to you.

I hunched over the bar and took a look see around at the guys in the booths and at the populated end of the bar. I was looking for three particular men—the one who would move first, the one carrying the most risk, and the one who looked like the richest mark. It was a good-luck evening for me; all three came in the same package.

"Care if I sit?" he asked, and before the phrase was completed, he'd already slid into the stool beside me. His hands were trembling; someone who was afraid of the consequences but just couldn't help himself. Someone I could control.

"Nope," I answered. I looked at him in the mirror behind the liquor shelves. Forties maybe. Pinstriped suit. Worked out a bit, but losing that battle—not too badly yet. Probably stuck to his desk sixty hours a week doing something important in this town of ultimate power. Manicured nails. I'd already noticed that—that and the obvious tailored cut of the fine-cloth suit—which had helped me put him at the top of the list. A nice smile and a sensuous mouth. He looked like he knew how to use that, given the right circumstances.

"Meeting someone?"

"Not that I know of," I answered. Then I decided to cut to the chase. I was still thinking of that milk-chocolate dancer back at the boat. Sean. I'd said I'd give him another opportunity at nine. It was after eight now. "Maybe it's you. If conditions are right," I said. Giving him a good smile back.

"I'd like that," he muttered under his breath. And I could tell he would; he was already breathing hard, and his answer had come out in a bit of a stutter.

"A hundred bucks," I said.

He hesitated. He wanted to think about it, but probably didn't want to leave that impression, and he didn't have the leisure to be in the hunt too long or too obviously. Going into a short stall, he motioned the barman over and had his Martini replaced. The barman used the best gin without asking. That might have been a mistake. Not only was the mark known here, but he also was known for buying the best. I was originally thinking of $100 as a starting price to work down from. Now I knew it could be the firm price.

"Well, I . . ."

"A hundred bucks," I repeated.

"There's the room and all . . ."

"This place has got an alley, doesn't it?" I said. I'd actually discovered that this excited them. And it made the possibilities more immediate.

"Well, I . . ." His voice was wavering. He looked confused and was wearing a sloppy grin. He reached down and adjusted something, taking pressure off his basket, something going on down there. He was hooked. The danger of me and where we would do it was meeting the fantasy that had brought him here.

I made him go down on his knees in the muck in the alley while he was sucking me off in the shadows next to a trash bin that should have been emptied last month sometime. Then I stood him against the slimy brick wall with his chest and cheek pressed to the bricks and his pelvis cantilevered out while I gave him a hundred bucks worth of cocking. He didn't complain about any of it.

Afterward I decided against going back into the bar. This was about what I'd figured on making to add to the escape kitty tonight, and I'd assumed I'd have to make more than one trip to the alley. But I got it in one. There seemed to be a whole lot more money in Washington, D.C., than there was in New York these days.

It was 8:45 and I knew I could make it back to the boat easily by 9:00. I walked slow and took a roundabout route, though, because I didn't want to be punctual and let the little fucker think I was panting after him. But if I thought about it too hard, I might have to admit to myself that I probably was panting after him. I hadn't been turned down like that since before I could remember. It made him intriguing. His loyalty to Masters sort of impressed me too, even though it was misplaced.

I saw him sitting there on the park bench at the top of the grassy incline, looking down into the lights of the yacht basin. His shoulders were hunched forward so that he looked like he'd imploded, collapsed inside himself. He still looked cute, and oh so fuckable. Maybe even more so now than before.

Before what? I asked myself. But I knew. I'd known before I left him on the *Boxoffice*'s fantail. He had no idea about Masters and Handelsman. That was clear. Seeing what I knew he was going to see if he stuck around the *Boxoffice* couldn't help but educate him real quick.

I walked over and stood by the bench. "You OK?"

Sean turned and looked up at me. He had tears in his eyes and it looked like he'd gained ten years in world knowledge and the entire globe had landed on his back since I'd last seen him. I sat down beside him on the bench and pivoted toward him. "What are you doing up here? Isn't it warmer down on the ship?" I knew the answer; I just wanted to start him talking. And I wanted him to talk to me, confide everything to me, and leave this bench with me. And beg me to fuck him. So I could do it and then put thoughts of him behind me.

"I . . . I couldn't."

"They're fucking, aren't they?" I asked. It was getting chilly out here. We needed to goose this along.

That loosened him up, and he began to tell me he'd seen Masters fucking Lenny in Lenny's "special" cabin. Even though I knew it, it still hit me hard when I heard it confirmed. And it made me mad, too.

Then I thought I could cut my ire by really putting the moves on this little guy. I did that, making him tell me about him being he a dancer, even though I'd heard him tell Cersenka that in the meeting earlier, and that Masters had put the kibosh on that. We discussed how hard it was for a black man to make it in the theater just so that I could do a little bit of "it's me and you against the world" prep with him. And I got him to tell me he was practicing his dancing again because they were strapped for cash and Sean thought he'd have to carry more of the income load—of which I knew he hadn't told his Mr. Masters. I didn't like the sound of that. Handelsman wasn't strapped for cash. I could just see Masters muscling in on him to ride that gravy train. And then where would I be? Handelsman was *my* gravy train. I started adding up the current balance of my escape money in my mind.

And that's when Sean got under my skin. I'd been too cocky and had told him too much about the nature of my relationship with Handelsman and, probably because he felt wounded himself, the little fucker started razzing me about being Lenny's kept boy. It being the truth still wasn't what I wanted to hear from a little piece of fluff I wanted to get my cock into.

So, it ended up with me backing off from him and escaping—down the grassy incline and across the quay and up the gangplank onto the *Boxoffice*'s fantail.

If I'd seen Masters in the salon, I probably wouldn't have entered, I'd probably have gone around the outside deck to get to the sleeping cabins, but I already was in the salon when I heard him greet me. Quite jovial, quite satisfied with himself. Just like a guy who'd just gotten his rocks off, which undoubtedly fit here.

He was standing behind the bar in the salon, stirring up a couple of drinks. He was naked, as I could tell from seeing the backend of him in the mirror behind the bar. He was in very, very good shape for an old geezer.

"Drink?" he asked.

"No thanks, I'm driving," I answered. Wrong crack, though.

"Yes, Lenny tells me you have quite a driver," he said. "Care to join us?"

"You're not done?" I asked. I mean he looked in great shape, but, god, the man was in his fifties. How much stamina could he have? But then he walked from behind the bar, and I saw the pecker and set of nuts on him—he was still or again at least at half staff—and I took a deep breath. It was obvious he wasn't finished for the night. And it was equally obvious that he had championship equipment. That little faker, I thought of the cute little brother sitting up on the bench. He loved cock after all. He would have to to be able to take Masters' supersized pecker.

"If you want us, we'll be just across the wall," Masters said. And then, still smiling, he turned and strutted down the corridor.

It wasn't long before I heard Lenny moaning and groaning and crying out for the fuck. I couldn't tell if he seemed more excited than when I fucked him, but even having to try to compare was an insult—and a threat.

I sat and nursed a beer. And then another. And the noises didn't stop. What sort of superman was this Masters guy anyway, I thought. And I was beginning to have respect for him—at least for him as a fucking machine. And I couldn't help but have a twitch in my crotch. There had been a time when I'd died for cock like that too. Not for some time. But maybe it was like riding a bicycle.

I got up off the bar stool and strolled slowly into and down the corridor until I was standing at the doorway to the owner's stateroom. They didn't even have the sensitivity to shut the door.

Lenny was on his side on the bed, facing me, his hip propped up on a pillow, a look of ecstasy on his face that made me more than a bit envious—and jealous and threatened all at once. His upward leg was being held straight up by Masters, who was on his knees on the bed behind Lenny's butt and stroking Lenny's ass hard with his cock. Lenny was pulling on his own cock, and his eyes were slitted like he didn't see me in the doorway, which he probably didn't. He was moaning softly like a wind-up doll that was wearing down but just had a few more sounds to grind out.

Masters did see me and smiled big.

"Decided to join us?" he asked. His tone was mocking, self-assured. And if it hadn't been for that, I might have been drawn into the room. I had to give it to Masters. I could command a room when I entered it—but not like Masters could command a room. He was a bright light, a regular torch. I could understand how everyone around him felt like a moth. Because that was exactly how I felt. I'd taken cock in my rocky road to where I was now. But I hadn't taken cock since Lenny offered me a job—and a bed. But here I was speculating, wondering how it would be to take Masters' cock.

I did actually take one step in the room, and I had my hand on my basket. But then Masters laughed. A self-complaisant victory laugh. And that did it. I turned and left the room, crossed the corridor, entered one of the guest cabins, slammed the door shut behind me, and shot the lock.

Masters laughed again. And I couldn't help but compare the assurance behind his laugh to my own thoughts that I could have Sean Singleton's ass eventually—the self-assuredness that it wasn't an if but a when and that there was time enough to wait for it. And, much to my horror and chagrin, I couldn't see a bit of difference between the two of us.

I laid down on the bunk in the guest cabin and pulled a pillow over my head and waited for the moaning to stop so I could sleep. It wasn't that long afterward that I heard Masters leaving. I rose and went over to the cabin window and watched him slowly walk up the glassy incline to where Sean Singleton still was sitting, waiting for him, in the chilly night.

I half expected to see something dramatic out there, but I was disappointed in that. As Masters approached the bench, Singleton merely stood until Masters had swept by, not missing a step. And then Singleton dropped in step four paces behind his master and they crossed the road. I lost sight of them as they moved around the octagonal building that was the original Arena Stage hall.

I went back to the bunk and went into an exhausted sleep almost immediately. I was awakened shortly afterward by Lenny pounding on the cabin door.

"Is that where you are, Gil?" he called out. "Come to bed. He's gone. It's lonely over here."

I went back to the pillow-over-the-head stance. How Lenny could want me back in his bed tonight after the pounding he'd taken from Masters was beyond me. And he needed to be punished anyway. I needed to make some sort of statement before this got out of hand. Or did I? I began to add together all of the stashes I had hidden around. The money Lenny didn't know I was accumulating, because Lenny had no idea I was doing business on the side—that I was trying to pull together escape money. To escape Lenny and this demeaning life.

All went quiet. I couldn't go to sleep again, though, tired as I was. I wanted to punish Lenny. I wanted to hurt him, to let him know that he couldn't just push me aside like that just for old time's sake. And worse, that he couldn't make it so obvious that he liked that old buzzard's cocking as much as he liked mine.

Punish him. Make him hurt.

In the end there was really only one way to do that. I got up off the bunk, stripped down, and worked my cock up hard—making it easy by imagining taking that cute little ass on Masters' assistant, Sean—a double victory: conquering the nice little milk-chocolate piece and cuckolding Masters at the same time. When I was ready, I unlocked the cabin door and pulled it open. I quietly crossed the corridor and entered the owner's stateroom.

Lenny was asleep, on his belly, naked and on top of the sheets. Snoring up a storm.

I swiftly moved up on the bed, got his hips between my knees, thrust my cock deep inside his now-gaping channel, and rode him hard, intent on punishing him for embarrassing me and bringing that maddening Creighton Masters into our lives and conflicting me as he did. And getting madder by the moment—because Lenny was very much awake now and letting me know that he was thoroughly enjoying the fucking.

Chapter Four: Sean

I slept very poorly because of what was going on over my head in the loft bedroom. I'd stayed late at the theater, mostly in the hope that they'd be finished for the night before I came back to the 7th Street townhouse, but they were just getting started good then. All of that grunting and groaning. I knew that Mr. Masters was giving it to him good. I could almost feel every deep thrust, hear every answering groan and moan, as if it was coming from me. So often it was. I knew just how it felt to be power fucked by the great playwright, Creighton Masters.

And I missed it whenever it wasn't me.

We were four weeks into the stage rehearsals of *Defiance*, and we, Mr. Masters and I . . . well, OK, *I* was in that process of readjusting the scripted wording and movement on the stage to meld naturally to the actual actors performing the work and to the director, Leonard Handelsman's, changes of the blocking—the who stands where when—of the staging to meet the special needs of theater in the round.

This was all a convoluted process that few realized a stage production went through—this adjusting of the written script to meld with a particular production of the play. And the process this time was almost farcical. Handelsman sat in the third row of the theater and put the actors through their paces. Most of them still had scripts in hand, but we were getting close to the "scripts down" rehearsal stage, and most of the actors were weaning themselves away from these props already. The end of this stage would also pretty much finish the need for me—and for Mr. Masters, for that matter—although the playwright would, of course, remain lounging at the back of the theater, basking in the beauty of "his" lines, scowling occasionally when he thought a golden line had been swallowed, clearing his throat when Handelsman—or anyone else—made a suggestion that sullied "his" brilliant prose, and otherwise making himself insufferable to the director, who, when he then was being mastered by the playwright in the bedroom, could deny him nothing.

It was this period during which I wasn't so much impressed with Mr. Masters—watching him prance around and take credit for work I did.

Mr. Masters sat three rows behind Handelsman and to the side far enough that Handelsman only needed to turn his head to consult. Mr. Masters' function was to take notes on changes Handelsman was requesting in the scripting as he went along for a complete rework of that portion of the script overnight to be available for another run-through the next day. At least that was the theory of what Mr. Masters was doing. In reality, he was doodling on his pad, drawing fanciful castles in the air, while I, sitting just behind him and to his side, was taking the real notes. Because it was I who was going to be staying late that evening to recast and recopy the script pages for the morning. Mr. Masters hadn't polished or recast—or even wordsmithed—his scripts since he had taken me under his wing and into his bed three years earlier.

Sitting at the back of the theater all of this time, brooding and just watching the rest of us interact, was the hulking Gil Johnson, Handelsman's assistant. I found him particularly disconcerting, because sometimes when there was a break in the note taking, I would glance back and up to the upper levels of the seating, and he'd be watching me. Every time. I found it both flattering and scary. I'd done my best to let him know my loyalties were fully with Mr. Masters. But he didn't care. He always seemed to be watching me and always seemed to be making clear that there was some unfinished business between us.

I found that particularly confusing and frustrating considering how relationships around here had shaken out.

As usual, last evening the rehearsal went late. I had rather more changes to make in the script than I had anticipated. Mr. Masters and Handelsman didn't even bother to suggest that I join them at the Flagship restaurant over on the waterfront before retiring to the *Boxoffice* for their after-dinner brandies and cigars before the rest of our typical night around here unfolded. Gil gave me an apologetic look and walked out behind them.

When I was alone, I gathered up all of my notes and walked through the maze of corridors backstage, which, this being a theater in the round, actually swirled around the stage under the raised seating, until I reached Handelsman's office. This was a dressing room he'd just more or less taken over without any sort of formal assignment. It would revert to a dressing room when the actual performances started, at which time the director is pretty much superfluous unless the opening night reviews point to flaws that can be easily fixed by recasting of this or that. At this point, both the director and playwright might have to go into furious brainstorming and work again.

Since Handelsman's tenure was temporary, the dressing table had become his desk, and the costume racks and chaise lounge for settling a principal actor's nerves were just pushed off to the side.

With a sigh, I settled down in front of my laptop computer that I had perched on the dressing table and brought up the existing script side by side with the notes I'd been tapping in over the five-hour rehearsal.

"I brought you a sandwich and a Coke."

The deep baritone voice surprised me, and I gave a little cry and turned to the door.

"Thanks . . . thanks, Gil," I said, "That was thoughtful." I realized my tone was a little icy. It was, in fact, a thoughtful thing for him to do . . . a very nice thing. This was all just so awkward—especially after what he had told me he felt—and what I'd told him I felt.

He walked over and put the aluminum foil-wrapped sandwich and the can of Coke, beaded with cold sweat, on the top of the dressing table next to the laptop and then moved his hand to where his fingers were lightly pressing on my forearm.

"Sean . . . I'm sorry. I—"

"I have more work to do here than I thought I would, Gil. Thanks for the food. That . . . that was very thoughtful. But don't you have someplace you need to be?"

He retracted his fingers. They had felt like hot pokers. I was glad he'd backed off. But, who was I fooling? No, I wasn't really glad he backed off.

I started to say something, but I couldn't really think of what to say. And it didn't matter anyway, because when I turned toward the door, he was gone.

I soldiered on, the rewrites taking twice as long as I anticipated, because I couldn't take my mind off Gil. He had tried to say something. He had wanted to talk about it, but I'd cut him off. Eventually, of course, something had to be talked about. Someone had to say something. This was all becoming so convoluted—and so out of the character of anything I had imagined.

It was after midnight before I got back to the townhouse. So, I thought the place would be quiet. It was uncomfortable enough to have to sleep on the sofa downstairs—where I'd been sleeping for a week already. But it was impossible to sleep hearing the sounds from upstairs.

Still, I must have gotten some sleep, because they woke me up the next morning—late, as usual. None of us were morning people—as they clattered down the staircase in the high-ceilinged living room and started scrounging around in the kitchen for something to quell the hunger that all-night fucking built up.

"Did you finish the rewrites?" That was all Mr. Masters said. He didn't ask if the sofa was uncomfortable or if I minded being displaced from my place in his bed or if I minded that he fucked someone else just above my head when he had insisted on exclusivity for both of us. He was the lion of the theater, the great playwright. And he didn't owe anyone explanations. Certainly not me. And I wasn't being snide. I understood how it was with us and what my role in his life was. This wasn't the first time since I'd been with him that he had gone off sniffing at some other tail he wanted.

That didn't mean I had to like it.

"Yes," I answered, as I stood up from the sofa and scrunched my back, trying to get it back into alignment. "Everything's on the table in the director's office. Copies for everyone, including the actors and lighting man."

"Good. I'm going to the theater and put in my appearance," Mr. Masters said. And then he was gone. No sense of embarrassment or apology for his behavior—for his need for instant gratification anywhere he sought it and anyone he wished to exploit to get it.

And still I loved him. He was the greatest playwright of the living theater, and I was in awe of the privilege to serve him.

But now, as I watched him walk away from me and out of the door, not a care in the world, the only word I could think of him as was "bastard."

"Sean . . . I . . . I'm sorry."

I turned on Gil, ready to let loose all of my ire and hurt on him. But he was sitting there, at the kitchen counter, wearing nothing but sleeping shorts, his heavy cock and balls peeking through the open fly, having lain under Mr. Masters and been fucked through the night, and, despite him having displaced me from my bed, I couldn't hate him. It wasn't just that he was beautiful. Big and black and muscled and sexy and handsome as he could be. It was because I knew it wasn't his fault.

"I don't know—"

58

"I didn't know why *I* gave in to him either," I said, cutting in on whatever apology Gil was going to give me. He didn't owe me anything, not really. It wasn't as if he and I meant anything to each other.

Easy to think or say. But still, there was some deep hurt inside me, and it wasn't only because Creighton Masters was being Creighton Masters. Any illusions I might have had about Creighton Masters had slowly but surely been stripped away over the years. But as long as he was the master playwright . . .

But then, almost as if he read my mind, Gil changed the subject.

"You've been working every night. And Creigh . . . well, Creigh hasn't been."

I looked sharply at Gil, and at least he had the decency to look sheepish. Of course Mr. Masters hadn't been working the last week of nights. He'd been screwing Gil. I could only imagine what Leonard Handelsman thought of this. Gil was supposed to be screwing him. But Handelsman hadn't been showing any signs of anger. And he took long lunch hours—and took Gil with him back to the *Boxoffice* for those. So, I assumed Handelsman was getting his balling as well. Gill Johnson apparently was quite a busy boy.

"And so?" I asked.

"And so, it's you who are doing the script rewrites, isn't it?"

I didn't answer for a long moment, but then I decided there was no reason I couldn't admit it to Gil. "Yes, I've done the rewrites."

"How much of the writing have you done and for how long?"

The million-dollar question. Out in the air at last. "I do pretty much all of it," I answered. "But Mr. Masters still has the concept and the broad brush look. I just fill in the words."

"How many of the words . . . and for how long?" He certainly was a persistent bastard.

"Pretty much all of them, I guess," I answered. And then because he'd asked it twice and probably would continue asking until I answered. "And for the three years I've been with him."

"That would mean, in terms of plays?"

"The last two . . . well, the last three, counting *Defiance*," I answered.

"In other words, all of the plays credited to his comeback phase," Gil said. His tone was flat, and it wasn't a question.

I didn't respond, so after a moment, he spoken again. "And you've stuck with him."

"The genius is still there," I answered, my chin set, my fists bunched up. Somebody had to defend the lion of the theater. "He'll come back. He just needs confidence. This staging of *Defiance* is just the thing."

"And if it isn't?" Gil said softly. "And if he doesn't come back after *Defiance,* how much longer will you—?"

"He will," I shot back, and then I added. "I'm sure he will . . . but as long as it takes, I guess."

I turned and started up the stairs to take my bath, now that I wouldn't need to be walking over fucking bodies.

"Somebody needs to tell Lenny," Gil said, still softly, to my retreating back. "If you won't tell

Handelsman, I think I must. I have professional responsibilities too."

"I don't see that it matters," I turned and said, eyes flashing. "Handelsman is getting the script he wants. He hasn't complained. He's salivated all over Mr. Masters on the high quality of the script—through the changes."

"Still . . ."

"And what makes you think he doesn't already know?" I asked. But before Gil could respond to that, I hurried up the stairs and into the bathroom.

When I came back downstairs, Gil was gone. And he'd washed up after Mr. Masters and himself. At least he'd spared me that indignity.

I wouldn't be needed at the theater now until after the noon hour. Mr. Masters and Handelsman would be closeted with the dance master, Miloslav Cersenka, discussing the integration of the dream dance sequences into the fabric of the play as it was being recast.

I didn't want to be there for that, and Mr. Masters had excused me, with a knowing smile, although I don't know what it is he thought he knew. He likely knew I hadn't abandoned my love for the dance and was frustrated at having a dance master of the caliber of Cersenka at hand without the opportunity of working with him. Even if so, Mr. Masters didn't know that I was continuing to practice for the day when I might have to earn much of our daily bread.

With that in mind I began clearing the furniture to one side in the living room of the 7th Street townhouse. I was lucky in that the townhouse had wonderful highly polished oak floors. I also was lucky that the banister of the staircase wrapped around in an embellishment on the first floor that gave me a near-perfect barre position—a railing at a good height to hold onto as I did my practice warm-ups.

I put a recording on the CD player and started through the five basic positions, limbering up for the more difficult positions to follow.

My thoughts went to Cersenka and the maddening knowledge that he wanted me for the *Defiance* dance troupe—or at least said he wanted me.

I had taken the opportunity—or made the mistake, I'm not sure which fit best—of attending one of his early audition sessions. He would only select one final candidate at each audition, which would seem strange to those who didn't know that full control, full dedication to him was one of the prices of a successful audition.

He walked into a room with some twenty dancers in it on that audition day. It was early in the audition cycle, and several of them would ultimately be picked for the troupe. But only one on this day. Never two on the same day.

I was sitting apart from the others, those trying out for the troupe, but when Cersenka tapped into the room, using his ivory-headed cane to lean on and looking as gaunt as he had on that first meeting I had attended in this practice room—gaunt but rangy, with sinewy muscles and handsome, hollow-cheeked face—he surprised me. He walked halfway down the length of the room, with its polished wood floor and bereft of any furniture other than the practice piano and a scattering of folding chairs, none of which were occupied by the dancers. All of the dancers were striking a pose, hoping to be noticed by the famous dance master.

But I was sitting and Cersenka stopped beside my chair and looked down into my now-upraised face. "Mr. Singleton, isn't it? Creigh Masters' Mr. Singleton?"

"Yes," I answered, impressed he had made the effort to find out who I was.

"Are you here to audition, Mr. Singleton?"

"No, just to watch the audition . . . if I may," I answered.

"Of course. But you are still a dancer, aren't you, Mr. Singleton? You still have your form, the walk."

"Yes," I answered. "But there really has been no time to keep up with it. Mr. Masters keeps me—"

"Yes, I know what Mr. Masters keeps you doing, young man," Cersenka said. And then he voiced something between a sniff and a snort.

"But you look like you live to dance to me. Should you ever want to audition, I'm interested. Yes, I'm definitely interested."

I blushed and lowered my head and thanked him, and Cersenka tapped beyond me and organized his audition rota.

I was embarrassed, because I fully understood what Cersenka was offering. I was sure the rumors were true. And they did prove to be true on this day.

Cersenka only made it through eight dancers when he saw something in a young, red-headed woman that he thought would be suitable for *Defiance*. He whispered a few sentences to her, and she nodded her head like she understood and accepted what he was saying. He told the seven dancers who had already auditioned unsuccessfully for him that they were released. But he told the others they were free to attend the next audition. I left him standing there with the young woman dancer and filed out with the rest.

After checking in at the stage, however, to see if Mr. Masters wanted me for anything, I was sent to Handelsman's office to retrieve some lighting charts he'd left in there. My journey took me by the door of the dressing room Miloslav Cersenka was using, and I heard the unmistakable sounds of sex on the other side of the door. Just as I had been told, Cersenka was applying the last element of the audition to the young lady. In ensuing days, I saw that she had made the troupe.

My limbering-up exercises finished, I moved out to the cleared space and went up on my toes demi-pointe and practiced some of the more challenging positions. Today I concentrated on my glissades and the twirling fouetté en tournant, practicing the latter until I almost was dizzy and falling to the floor. I was pleased. In spite of the lack of sleep and the cramped sleeping position, I had done them well.

When I got to the theater, the actors were finishing up a run-through of act 1, scene 2, and Handelsman seemed pleased. There had been a lot of rewriting to do on this section of the scene the previous evening, and I hadn't been given very good directions on how to change the wording. I had to do a lot of my own interpretation of what Handelsman had wanted. So, I was particularly pleased when he turned and raised a "thumbs up" to Mr. Masters, with a broad smile.

When I arrived, the senior lighting technician had a long ladder set up at one edge of the stage, and

Gil was holding it steady while the guy was up in the rafters over the stage, resetting some lights. When he came down the ladder, Gil didn't move away at once, and the lighting technician, who was perhaps in his late thirties and a bit on the pudgy side, was on the lower ladder rungs, inside Gil's arms, while they whispered to each other for a couple of minutes. Then the ladder was lowered, and Gil helped the lighting guy take it down one of the four ramps that led beside and then under the seating down from the circular arena stage into backstage area.

Not long after that Handelsman sent me to his dressing room for some papers, and I heard the sounds of taking beyond the open door of one of the dressing rooms. The long ladder was propped up along the corridor wall. I looked in, and the lighting technician's belly was hanging over the back of a chair, and his jeans were down around his knees, and Gil was standing between his legs and pumping his channel with an impressive brown cock.

I hurried on, both flustered and disturbed by what I saw. I didn't condemn Gil for getting it anywhere he could—or, more likely, the lighting technician getting it wherever he could. But he hadn't earned any respect from me for what he was doing. Worse, though, I was disturbed that my first reaction was one of envy—of wishing it had been me bent over that chair back.

I was barely back in the theater and seated behind Mr. Masters, when both he and Handelsman were rising. The actors were clearing the stage. I wondered why the rehearsal had been called; it barely had begun. Or maybe they were just taking a break.

But Mr. Masters came out to the aisle and started up to the back of the theater, where the exits were. I moved to follow him, but Handelsman's voice rang out.

"Could you come to my office with me, Sean? I have something to go over with you there."

I looked quizzically at Mr. Masters, but he just turned to me and spread his arms and shrugged. Obviously he wanted me to go with Handelsman.

When we entered Handelsman's office, I went in first. He followed, shutting the door and leaning up against it.

"We could go over the notes for script changes from today's rehearsal, Sean," Handelsman said.

I went into a panic. As far as I knew, there wasn't much of a rehearsal. I'd been on time, but the rehearsal had already started—and it stopped shortly after I'd come back from retrieving some papers from this office for Handelsman. I didn't have any notes to go over.

"Huh, notes?" I asked to stall. "Shouldn't Mr. Masters be here if you want to go over the notes?" Maybe since I wasn't around, Mr. Masters had made some notes, I thought—and hoped.

"Why should Creigh be here, Sean?" Handelsman asked. "I understand you are the one who actually rewrites the scripts at night."

Oh god, I thought. Gil had told him. Dammit.

"Mr. Handelsman—" I started to say. But I couldn't think of anything to say.

"And I understand that Creigh has been fucking my Gil," Handelsman said.

"What? I don't know how that . . . I don't know—"

"We have a basic problem, here, Sean," Handelsman said. He was smiling at me—assessing me. "There's something pretty newsworthy—that Creigh Masters' plays haven't been Creigh Masters' plays for some time, at least since his popularity has resurged. And there's something of more personal concern to me. I haven't been getting enough because Creigh Masters has been poking my lover. Now, how do you think those two things fit together, Sean? And what do you think we could do to smooth that over?"

"I don't know . . . I—" He was moving entirely too fast for me.

"I understand you are devoted to Creigh Masters, Sean. Is that true?"

"Yes," I said in a low voice. I couldn't look at him now. I was pressed to the opposite wall, looking at my feet.

"And you'd do anything to save Creigh Masters' reputation, wouldn't you, Sean?"

"Yes," I said, although I took a little longer to answer this time.

"You know I've fancied you since that first day you came into the meeting in the dance studio," Handelsman said. His voice was thick now, hoarse and low.

"No, no, I didn't imagine . . . Mr. Handelsman . . ."

"Would you be comfortable with me taking your clothes off for you, Sean, or would you like to do that yourself?"

Handelsman fucked me while sitting on the edge of the chaise lounge at the back of his office. I sat on his cock facing away from him, and staring at what we were doing in the mirror above the dressing table he was using as a desk—until I couldn't take the shame anymore. Then I just let my head hang and counted the squares in the linoleum on the floor.

He wasn't particularly big, and he took me slowly. He had his arms wrapped around my torso and one hand playing with my nipples and the other pumping my cock off, while, at his direction, I rose and fell on his erection. He had his face buried in the hollow of my neck from the back and hummed me a lullaby as we fucked, first to my ejaculation, and then to his, filling out the bulb of a condom inside my channel.

All the time he was fucking me, he was murmuring how nice I was, how much he'd wanted me for weeks, and how alive I made him feel.

I was crying softly, not the least because—pathetically—this was the most affection I'd had in three years.

In the end, after we'd come, he turned my face to his and kissed the tears on my cheek and then my lips.

"That was nice, very nice," He whispered. "We will have to do this every day."

"Mr. Masters," I choked out. "I've pledged."

"Shush, little one," he murmured. "You are doing this for Mr. Masters. In time, though, I hope you will be doing this for us."

"But . . . but," I whispered. "What if he ever found out?"

Handelsman gave a low, dry laugh. "What makes you think he doesn't know? Why do you think he left you with me this afternoon?"

I said nothing about my meeting with Handelsman when I returned late that afternoon to the 7th Street townhouse after the director had given me another lesson in director couching, laying me on my back on the chaise lounge with my legs open to him as he scooted his knees under my buttocks and fucked me slowly and as sensuously as I ever could have hoped that Mr. Masters would—and didn't.

Mr. Masters asked nothing about the long, private meeting either, which, I guess, was enough for me to be at least suspicious about what Mr. Masters knew of Handelsman's intent.

"Come see if you can make heads or tails of these bills, Sean," he called out to me from the desk in the living room as I entered the townhouse.

I was somewhat taken aback, because I handled all the bills. I wasn't even aware he knew where I kept them.

I sighed and walked over to the desk. "I've been meaning to talk to you about those, Mr. Masters. But you've been so . . . busy of recent evenings."

"Well, we're all alone tonight," he said, and he smiled up at me. It was his "I want to be serviced" smile.

I gave him a confused look.

"Gil isn't here tonight," he said. "I've told him not to come over tonight. It's just the two of us. You can sleep upstairs again tonight."

A sense of relief flooded into me. I hated facing him after what I'd done with Handelsman, even if I'd done it to protect him. But maybe the thing with Gil was over; maybe we could get back to normalcy now.

"The bills," I said. "What they mean is that we'll have to really cut back—at least until a check comes through on the *Defiance* production. And maybe . . . maybe it's time to start thinking about the next script. I . . . I have something written, if you'd like to take a look at it."

He ignored my offer of another script and continued on another track of his own. "You know I'm sure Miloslav would like you for the dance troupe for this production." He'd said it quietly, as if he was testing the waters, as if he hadn't really let that elephant out into the room.

"Are you saying—?" I was flabbergasted, floored. Mr. Masters knew what Miloslav Cersenka demanded of his dancers. And he'd been adamant about my staying away from the dance—and not fucking with other men. I was doubly floored. But the casual way he was suggesting I give myself to Cersenka after all he'd demanded about exclusiveness—added to the possibility that he had given me to Handelsman as well. Well, I was speechless. At least for the moment.

"I'm saying we need money, and the dancing troupe will be paid well. And I know you've been practicing for the possibility of returning to the stage. I'm saying you could help pay the bills if you wanted to."

He even knew I'd been practicing. I staggered to a chair and sat down. But he was standing up as I sat down.

"Come, let's go upstairs," he said. And he held his hand out to me. "I've told Gil to go to the boat tonight. I want you tonight."

Mr. Masters' fucking was rough and dominating in contrast to the lovemaking of Handelsman earlier that afternoon. And his dick was massive in both length and thickness in relationship to Handelsman. He covered me with his heavy body and was thrusting into me, insistently, before I was quite ready for him. My cries and groans aroused him even more, and he devoured me with his body, with his personal need. It was all about him. And I responded in kind, melding to it being all about him. Listening for his moan or his sigh or for a simple "yes" from him and then adjusting to what he wanted. Opening to him, surrendering my all, moving my hips to the rhythm of him long after I was well past exhaustion. Giving him whatever he wanted.

Long about the time the sun was only then setting outside the plate-glass window overlooking the envelope-sized back garden, Mr. Masters, both of us having ejaculated, held me close in his arms, his cock deep inside me, recovering, him already having promised that what we'd done so far was just a preliminary. And me believing him, having been here before.

In that brief interlude between fucks, where I was panting heavily and knew I'd be feeling his cock stir again inside me well before I was ready to resume taking him, he leaned his lips in to my ear and whispered, in a low, hoarse voice, "And, so, does Lenny Handelsman fuck you as good as I do?"

Chapter Five: Gil

I hadn't planned on letting Masters get to me—it was perhaps the last thing I'd ever say I'd do. He didn't fool me a bit, the pompous, egotistical user. But there was a reason he was able to bend so many to his will. He had charisma. He also had a championship dick and could fuck like no one else I'd ever met.

I only found that out by a crooked route, though. One night, three weeks into rehearsals for *Defiance* at Arena Stage, I came back aboard the *Boxoffice* late in the evening, having spent a couple of hours on the prowl, building up my escape fund at the expense of horny men at the Bachelor Pad who wanted a bit of what I could give. The boat was deserted from fantail through the main salon. I have no idea where Creighton Masters had been lurking. When I got to the owner's stateroom, however, Lenny was on the bed, naked. And, when he saw me in the doorway, he beckoned me to come onto the bed and earn my keep.

I'd actually been more than a little worried about where I stood in the earning-my-keep department, because Lenny had been spending much of his fucking time—and, yes, I mean that literally—with Masters. I got the distinct impression I was being forced out. And I felt like I still hadn't saved up enough money on the side to make my escape from this life. I don't want to even start getting into the wounded pride bit. But there was that too. Masters was a good thirty years older than I was. The very idea of having to compete with him burnt me to a crisp—little did I know then just how fucking good he was.

Anyway, I was there on top of Handelsman, having dragged him to the foot of the bed and made him stand on the floor there, bent over the bed, and I was servicing him deep and in rapid strokes, when I suddenly felt a hand palming my belly and the thick fingers of another one greased up and forcing themselves into my asshole.

I turned my head and saw that it was Masters and that he was naked. He and Handelsman must have already been at it and Masters had wandered off somewhere before I got there and come back, seen I'd arrived in Handelsman's asshole, and decided he wanted to play too.

I made threatening, growling noises to warn Masters off.

"Ride with it Gil," Handelsman muttered through clinched teeth. "It turns me on." I was being reminded who paid my bills.

"Well, it don't turn me on, Lenny. Get your fucking fingers out of there, Masters."

Masters laughed at that, and when I think of it now, I have to laugh too. Fucking me with his fingers was exactly what he was doing. But I didn't think it was all that funny at the time.

Lenny just hissed "behave" between groans, and my position with Lenny was too precarious to challenge that demand.

Within minutes, though, I was beyond caring—or complaining. Once Masters got his cock inside me and began to perform his magic, I was lost. I could understand now why Sean was so willing to put up with his dominating crap. The man had some of the best fuck techniques I'd ever felt.

Sometime during the next hour, Lenny had disappeared altogether, and it was just Masters and me, Masters working me like the master he was.

Then Lenny returned to bed, and we spent the rest of the night together, entwined in each other's arms and workin' our hips in unison from time to time.

My first regret when I woke up the next morning—not my only regret, because I wasn't so gaga over Masters' cock that I didn't regret being caught up in that particular whirlpool—my first regret was for Sean. That I was now muscling in on his food bowl just as I had been fearing Masters was muscling in on mine. And I still had a twinge of regret toward Sean when I reasoned my way out of that, telling myself that Sean was quickly becoming the moneymaker of that pair and that he deserved better than Masters. And maybe he'd see that in Masters hooking up with me, and I could be the conduit for him escaping his situation. But when I still couldn't shake the regret, I realized I had to start thinking about my own feelings toward Sean—just protective, or did it go farther than that?

That was the first full night that Masters had stayed away from the 7th Street townhouse. Sean had certainly looked perplexed the next afternoon when he arrived at the stage rehearsals and found Lenny and Masters there already, pretty as you please, no explanations from Masters on where he'd been all night. Sean, of course, knew where Masters had been. What he didn't know was that Masters had been with me on the boat and in Lenny's bed as well.

The big shock came then, five days later. By then the pattern had been established. Masters would come back to the *Boxoffice* while Sean was at the stage doing the script rewrites. Lenny and Masters would have drinks on the fantail and discuss the day's rehearsals, and then they'd have a late supper together in the salon. Lenny would leave Masters in the salon to drink his after-dinner brandy and smoke his cigar, and Lenny would retire to the owner's stateroom after knocking on the door of the cabin where I had been spending the evening, waiting to be summoned—or, if I'd gone out while they were having their drinks and supper to pick up a bit of tail that would pay for it and add to my escape fund, I jolly well needed to be back on the boat before Lenny retired.

I would go into the owner's stateroom with Lenny and fuck him for a while, and then Masters would appear and fuck me while I was fucking Lenny, and Lenny eventually would go off for a shower, leaving Masters still plowing me. That was part of the Masters' mystique—he could fuck for hours.

Except for the first night, though, Masters would end up going back to the townhouse.

But that fifth night, when I returned to the *Boxoffice*, Lenny was pouring two snifters of brandy and breaking out a set of cigars and proceeded to sit in a chair near where Masters was sitting and joined him in the brandy and smoke.

When I entered the salon, I saw the change in pattern and started back toward the corridor leading to the cabins.

"I'd prefer that you stayed, Gil," Lenny said. "In fact, please come over here and service Creigh's cock."

I stood there, shocked. I'd let Masters fuck me; I hadn't given him a blow job before. The guy had to be really something special for me to give him a blow job.

"I don't think so, Lenny," I said.

I don't know what had gone on between Lenny and Masters that was making Lenny act this way, but he was suddenly all hard assed.

"Do you like your job, Gil?" he asked. His voice was very cold.

"It's OK," I said. "Nothing I couldn't replace, though."

"Where do you go of evenings, Gil? When you leave here. Where could Jack have seen you, say two nights ago? And what could he have seen you doing?"

Jack was the head lighting guy at the theater. I thought maybe I'd seen him in the Bachelor Pad gay bar a couple of times. So this was it. This wasn't about Masters at all. This was about me and fucking with other men, men Lenny hadn't selected. This was punishment.

I could have brought it to a head, ignored Lenny's demand, not accepted the punishment, and seen if he was bluffing. Lenny never had it so good. He'd never had cocking to equal mine. Except, maybe, until Masters had come back into his life. And, now that I thought about it, he'd been with Masters before he employed me. Suddenly the balance wasn't looking all that much in my favor. And I didn't think I'd put together enough money yet to comfortably give up this job.

Also, I looked at Masters, and he had his cock out of his fly and was holding it up for me to see in all its glory. That was a little hard to deny as well.

I went over and knelt in front of Masters and sucked him off, as Lenny and Masters leaned into each other and kissed and cooed.

When I was done with Masters, I started back toward the cabins again, but they weren't finished with me.

"You're going with Creigh tonight, Gil," Lenny said in a soft voice that still had a hard tone to it.

"Lenny—" I started. But I saw the hard look in his eyes, and Masters was standing and holding a hand out.

Sean hadn't returned from the theater when we arrived at the 7th Street townhouse, and so the first he knew that Masters was cocking me at all was when he came home and found us in Masters' bed—in his, Sean's, bed.

I almost died at the look on his face when he came into the room, and I hated myself when he turned and quietly went downstairs and began making up the sofa in the living room as a bed. But I hated Masters more.

For a couple of weeks after that, I would go back to the *Boxoffice* over lunch hours and do Lenny in his bed and then, at night, I'd be in Masters' bed being done by him.

The hate I had for Masters and what we did mounted in me, and it became virulent as I watched what this was doing to Sean. And then the morning Sean admitted to me that it was he who had been the resurgence in Masters' success in the theater, Sean who had been doing most of the work on the newer, better received scripts, I'd had enough.

That day, before stage rehearsals started, before Sean came to the theater, I told Lenny that Masters was a fraud, that he hadn't recouped his writing genius at all, and that Sean was the real writing genius now. And there, in front of Lenny, when Masters appeared in the theater, I told Masters that my days in his bed were over.

I had no idea what Lenny would do, but by now he'd apparently accomplished the punishment he wanted to inflict on me, and he'd probably gotten tired of sharing me with Masters, and the revelation—which he should have figured out himself—that Sean was the one responsible for the high quality of the play and the sustaining of that quality through rewrites. And he said nothing when I lowered the boom on Masters.

Masters, the egotist that he was, also said nothing. He just laughed it off—played like I wasn't anything to him anyway and he'd only been fucking me in his bed because Lenny had said he wanted it to be that way. Before he'd left the building, I'm sure he'd convinced himself he was the one who cut it off with me.

Later I made sure that I had a nice little chat with Jack, the senior lighting technician. I couldn't blame him, really; he owed me nothing, and he owed Lenny everything. He probably thought he was doing the right thing for Lenny. And maybe it only didn't look right as seen from my perspective.

I was holding the long ladder for him while he was adjusting lights above the stage after the rehearsal had started. Lenny wanted to see how the actors were highlighted in the lights at several points of the stage to serve his blocking concepts—and he'd said this would be the extent of the rehearsal that day, that he was giving the actors the rest of the afternoon off.

When Jack came down the ladder, I didn't move away, and he came down more or less inside my embrace. He was mortified when I told him I knew he'd sussed me out to Lenny on my visits to the Bachelor Pad.

"God, Gil, I am so sorry. I just mentioned it in passing. I had no idea Lenny didn't know you went there . . . I . . . I . . . oh, god, Gil, I wouldn't do that to you on purpose for anything. I—"

It hit me then that Jack had the hots for me—probably enough that it was true he wouldn't have ratted me out to Lenny on purpose. And Jack had been in the Bachelor Pad too, or he wouldn't have seen me there. Jack wanted me. I leaned in closer to him, more intimately. Out of the blue, I'd had an idea. I felt so miserable about Sean, and I'd already thought a hundred times that I could escape to someplace like the Bachelor Pad to blow off the frustration of this four-cornered sex thing we were having with Masters and Handelsman—but Sean hadn't had a day away from this ever.

"You said you saw me in the Bachelor Pad, Jack?" I asked. I was palming the small of his back with one of my hands, and I let that wander down to his buttocks, as I so often did as my signal of interest. "What were you doing in the Bachelor Pad?" I asked.

"Same thing you were, Gil," Jack said. He stammered this out, but he was looking at me like he wanted to eat me alive.

And then, when I suggested we might make a little trip back stage if he did me a favor—and that I'd certainly forget about anything he said to Lenny getting me in trouble—I let him do just that. We went back to one of the dressing rooms, bumping off the stage, carrying the long ladder together, natural as you please, and leaving it outside the dressing room door, running up the side of the corridor. And then I unzipped my jeans and pushed him down on his knees in front of me and gagged him with my cock. He loved it. And after that, I bent him over a chair and fucked him. And he loved that too.

And at the end of the fuck session that he had been dreaming of and had no idea he'd ever get, he was more than willing to say that I could borrow his Mustang convertible anytime I wanted to.

We went to lunch then—in Jack's Mustang—and we ended up at his small apartment across the river in Rosslyn, where I fucked him again in his own bed just to make sure his loyalties would be to me, not Lenny. When I did borrow his car, I didn't want him telling Lenny I had it.

When I returned to the theater, I found the stage deserted. Lenny had carried through with his promise and released the actors. I entered through a stage entrance and I just walked on through the theater and up the elevated rows of seating and out into the lobby. Masters was there, preparing to leave out the front door. He turned as he heard me call out to him.

"The rehearsal broken up?" I asked. There was something unusual about seeing Masters in the lobby.

"Yes," he said. He was giving me a smile, a strange smile, as if there was some joke I wasn't privy too.

"Have you seen Lenny?" I asked. "Do you know if he's gone back to the *Boxoffice*?"

"No, I'm fairly certain he's still here," Masters said. And then he chuckled. I had no idea what he thought was so fuckin' amusing.

And then it hit me, what was unusual. Sean wasn't in tow. He was always there, walking a few paces behind Masters and carrying all of Masters' stuff. At least whenever Masters hadn't sent him off somewhere. But here was Masters, leaving the theater, carrying his own briefcase and water bottle and sweater. And Sean wasn't here.

"Where's Sean?" I asked.

Masters didn't answer. He just gave me that "I've got an amusing secret" smile. My blood turned to ice. And as Masters turned and opened the door to the chilly wind blowing up Maine Avenue, I swiveled, ducked into the darkened theater, and raced down the aisle and across the stage and onto one of the ramps running down into the backstage area.

I opened the door to Lenny's office, and there they were. Lenny, gazing over Sean's shoulder, his eyes slitted in lust, saw me and smiled. But Sean had his head bowed, looking at the floor, head and arms just hanging listlessly as he sat in Lenny's lap, facing me on the edge of the chaise lounge, and Lenny raised and lowered Sean's small, beautiful body on his cock. Sean was naked, his clothes strewn on the dressing room floor, and he was moaning softly and emitting a snuffling sound that made me think he was also crying. Lenny wasn't naked; he was in his shirt and trousers, but his fly was open, permitting his impaling cock to skewer Sean's channel. Sean's body was perfectly formed, a well-muscled, dancer's body. But of a small size. He looked almost like a boy in contrast to Lenny's broad chest and the large hands he had wrapped around Sean's waist to permit him to work Sean's torso up and down on his cock.

I felt a moan rising in my own body—and my own cock hardening up in arousal—and I quietly stepped back and silently shut the door again. I turned, my back to the wall next to the door, trying to compose myself, trying to regularize my breath and to will my cock to behave. I was disgusted with myself. And I was mostly disgusted not because Sean was obviously being suborned into letting Lenny fuck him by some nasty understanding between Masters and Lenny, but rather because I wanted to be fucking Sean myself.

* * * *

I kept to my resolution and neither went to Masters' bed again after that or came close enough for him to touch me and override my resolve. And in an attempt to save Sean, I stuck close to Lenny and fucked him so often that I was sure he was perpetually exhausted and milked and couldn't take advantage of Sean again.

But I couldn't protect Sean against everyone— and I knew I couldn't protect him against me if I got half the chance to have him.

The day after I'd seen him in Lenny's office being worked by Lenny, I once more found him absent from the theater when I arrived late for the afternoon stage rehearsal.

I entered the row behind Lenny, which was three rows in front of where Masters was sitting, and I leaned over and whispered in Lenny's ear. "Where's Sean? You know now that you can't give recasting notes with just Masters here."

"This scene is well blocked; I don't plan on any changes," Lenny whispered back, not bothering to turn his head but a bit and not taking his eyes off the stage.

"So, where's Sean?" I asked again, that being the real question I wanted answered. "Do you know?"

"He's in the dance studio. Cersenka's auditioning him for a spot in the dance troupe for *Defiance*."

My blood was running cold again. I knew exactly what this meant. I knew as well as anyone that Cersenka controlled his dancers by dominating them sexually—that no audition with him would be successfully completed without taking Cersenka's cock.

I jerked my head around so that I could see Masters, sitting behind us. Lenny and I hadn't been whispering loud enough for him to hear us, but I knew he knew what I had asked. He was smiling that amused smile of his.

I jerked away and rose and moved swiftly down the side of the stage and down a ramp to the backstage area and then started into a run for the annex building that housed the dance studio, the very dance rehearsal hall where I had first seen Sean in what now seemed to be ages ago. It had been long enough, certainly, for me to change from seeing Sean as just another cute little piece of ass I would fuck and forget to seeing him as so much more—seeing him as a vulnerable young man being misused and taken advantage of, someone I owed protection to because I too had hurt him. And more than this, maybe. More than just the need to protect him. I didn't want to think what more than this I could be feeling—but I couldn't kid myself; there was more than just protecting him on my mind.

I heard discordant music coming from the practice piano as I approached the door to the dance studio. I pushed open the door and took two steps inside the room, and then halted and moved to the side and leaned back against the wall next to the door.

There were only two of them, and they didn't notice me from start to finish. The piano was against the opposite wall. There was a line of ballet costuming strewn haphazardly from the center of the dance floor back to the piano. Red leg warmers, a black ballet unitard, a man's dance belt.

The second half of the dance master, Miloslav Cersenka's, audition was in full blossom.

Sean's butt was playing the keys of the piano, and his back was arched against the back casing of the piano. I could see the heel of one of his hands dug into the keyboard at the bass clef end, and his other hand was wrapped around Cersenka's neck, both doing what they could to hold himself steady. His legs were spread and lifted up from around Cersenka's waist. His small feet were still clad in ballet shoes, and his toes were daintily pointed toward where I was standing. That's essentially all that I could see of Sean, although there wasn't a doubt in my mind that it was Sean.

Standing between Sean's spread legs and facing him was the backside of a wiry, sinewy-muscled dance master. His black, form-fitting leotards were pulled down around his knees, and he was naked above that. His muscles bulged and strained as his pelvis rocked back and forth and his butt cheeks contracted and expanded in advanced stages of the fuck. His arms were on either side of Sean's slight torso, and the heels of his hands were buried in the keyboard. One of his legs appeared stiffer than the other in the motion of the fuck, but, barring this and the discordant music being coaxed from the piano by Sean's buttocks bouncing up and down on the keyboard in the rhythm of the fuck, the two were making beautiful music together with their lithe, flexible, highly trained bodies.

From the harmony of grunts and groans and moanings, I felt assured that Sean was passing his audition into Cersenka's dance troupe.

There was nothing I could do here. I knew that it was Sean's dream to dance for Cersenka. And I knew that Sean was aware of what was required to do that. Masters may have thought this was just another indignity being forced on Sean for his own amusement and yet another manifestation of his control over Sean, but I saw it as more than that—I saw it as an act of defiance, as the start of Sean's liberation from Masters.

I could have turned and left. I should have turned and left. But I didn't. I leaned back against the wall, unzipped my jeans, pulled out my cock, and pumped it in the rhythm of the audition fuck, joining their coupling to the extent that I could. I was finished and gone before they were done.

* * * *

My plan to give Sean a bit of relief came three days later. The rich-bitch backers of the production were gathering for a lunch at the Willard Hotel, where they expected to see the director, playwright, and dance master they were paying such a lot of cash for on display. Not only were these guys out of our way for three hours in the middle of what was an unseasonably warm and gorgeous day, but neither Sean nor I had been invited to the party.

So I decided to make a party of our own.

I had a luncheon basket made up at the Gangplank restaurant, secured the use of Jack's Mustang convertible, and told Sean about the outing at the last possible minute, not entertaining any demur or indecision, Then we were off, using the suggestions Jack had made to me on the quickest route to scenic— and private—beauty, over a Potomac bridge and onto the George Washington Parkway, headed west. When we hit the Beltway, I jagged off onto route 193, a winding road, where the lush trees met over the roadway, and multimillionaire mansions peeked out behind dogwood and oak trees at two-hundred-foot intervals. This route, which put us instantly into the rolling Virginia countryside, led out to Great Falls, a network of rapids on the Potomac River above the capital city of Washington, D.C. The river itself was navigable higher than this, but only if you could get past the rapids. In the early years of the American republic, a consortium headed by George Washington himself had dug a canal on the Maryland side of these rapids to give access by boat to the upper Potomac. But that canal was a dry bed now.

The most glorious thing about Great Falls Park was the foliage and the rocks and the many very private nooks and crannies tucked alongside the trails and the river gorge itself.

The great weather had not been predicted, so we had the park almost to ourselves. I searched until I found the perfect spot, close enough to the river to hear the dull roar of the rapids and see glimpses of rushing water between the trees, but off the walking path, in a small, moss-covered dell surrounded by protecting granite outcroppings and verdant tree coverage.

I had no trouble discerning that I had guessed completely correctly—that Sean had been yearning to get out of the theater environment. I could see that he wanted to relax and enjoy something different.

I hadn't actually intended on making love to him here—I'd tried doing it in the car in the parking lot, but he made me wait, while promising it might happen— which just heightened my desire for him. He was relaxed and happy and vocal, and he only objected mildly and only at first, when, after we'd eaten the box lunches while sprawled out on a blanket and drunk the beers I'd brought along, I embraced him and we began to kiss.

He murmured his "we shouldn't be doing this" objections while I slowly unclothed him, covering all revealed flesh liberally with kisses. But he just lay there, panting, and looking up at me all wide-eyed and shuddering as I stood over him and stripped down, showing him how much I wanted him, how much I had to give to him.

And then, surprising even myself, I showed myself how much farther beyond just protector and brief fling I thought our relationship was moving by coming down to him and covering his face and neck and nipples and belly with kisses and then voluntarily lowering my mouth yet farther and making love to his cock and balls and channel entrance with my lips and teeth and tongue until, writhing and groaning and moaning and sighing under me, begging for what I would eventually bury deep inside him, he released his hot, milky nectar for me to devour.

After he had come for me, he was putty in my hands, just lying there, panting shallowly, his eyes slitted as he watched me, kneeling between his spread thighs, roll the condom on my cock. Then I just pushed my knees under his buttocks, raising his pelvis to me to provide a good angle for a deep slide, and wrapped my arms around his waist, pulling his torso off the ground. He arched back, his shoulder blades touching the ground, his arms trailing away from his body, hands touching the grass, and his head turned to the side, with a dreamy look in his eyes. He gave a little jerk as I entered him, but then was reduced to low moans and sighing as I slowly pumped him to an ejaculation.

Chapter Six: Sean

I was never more nervous than while I was waiting in the dance rehearsal hall, trying to keep up with small talk with the pianist, while I was waiting for Miloslav Cersenka for my audition to dance in *Defiance*. I was torn. I wanted to do this, and not just for the money I needed to help keep Mr. Masters' lifestyle afloat. I needed this for me too. I was beginning to dissolve into Mr. Masters. If there was ever going to be anything left of me that was me, I needed someplace that Mr. Masters couldn't go. For me, that was the world of the dance.

On the flip side, however, I was afraid of what was required to become part of Cersenka's troupe—and I remained shocked that Mr. Masters could just share me around like this. First Leonard Handelsman and now Cersenka. Mr. Masters had always been so adamant that there would be no one but him. I felt used and worthless. I consoled myself with the thought that Cersenka may be too ill to follow his custom. Over the weeks of early preparation for the opening of *Defiance* at the Arena Stage, his condition had noticeably weakened and, if anything, he looked even more cadaverous and gaunt than ever before.

In the days since I had asked for and been granted the audition, I had been sitting in on the dance rehearsals so that I could see what dance positions and routines were going to be used and I could concentrate my audition on those. What surprised me the most about those rehearsals was Cersenka's movement there. He would appear, tapping his ivory-headed cane on the floor as he favored one leg in his steps. But then the music would start and he would be out among the dancers, still the master of all in his flexibility and the grace of his movements as he gave instruction. I ached for him on how he would feel when the day came when he no longer could dance like that. And I thought that what appeared to be an acceleration in the progress of his disease probably was welcome to him—that he preferred death to life as a cripple after having been a premier dancer.

When Cersenka entered the rehearsal hall, I stood away from the piano, in the first position, and watched his pained progression to the center of the room from the door. He merely snapped his fingers and the piano music began. Then he gracefully extended his hand to me and put on the mere hint of a smile, and I began to move over the floor in the prescribed audition positions. I was so keyed up that I had to keep trying to make my mind a blank, to let my body do what it had been conditioned and trained to do. It meant the world to me to do well, even though it frightened me to the core on where doing well would lead.

Cersenka was bare chested and bare footed, clad only in a form-fitting black leotard. Even in his emaciated state, his muscle tone held, and his veins popped out on his chest and arms, indicating there was practically no fat on his body for them to run through. He appeared made of steel.

At length I had come near him, and he commanded me to take the position of the arabesque penchée, where I lifted one leg high behind me at over a 90-degree angle and moved my torso forward, toward the floor, to counterbalance. Cersenka came close to me then and put one hand on my belly and the other one high on my thigh.

"Demi-pointe," he commanded. And, as directed, I went up on my toe. Cersenka, in dramatic strides, walked around in a circle, turning me. His breathing was raspy, and I felt the hand he had on my thigh move up and cup my basket.

I knew now that I had passed the dancing segment of the audition and we were now in the second phase—the phase where he possessed me as his.

"Felix, enough, thanks. You may go."

Cersenka was addressing the piano player, who brought the music to a graceful conclusion and stood up, bowed, and walked out of the rehearsal hall in long strides, my heart matching the beat of his clicking heels.

I was alone with Cersenka now. He was breathing heavily, and it wasn't all a result of his condition. I was trembling from the feel of his strong hand cupping my cock and balls through the tight-fitting unitard material and the dancer's belt.

He was still circling around in the center of the hall, moving me in the arabesque position. I felt his hand going from my basket up my extended leg, and he was pushing the red terry cloth leg warmer off my calf.

"Change position, arabesque penchée," he barked, and I came down off toe and lifted the other leg up as high as the first one had been and went back on demi-pointe. Cersenka circled me about a few more turns and then ran his hand up the extended leg and pushed the other leg warmer off.

His hands went to my shoulders, and he pulled the straps of the torso portion of my unitard down over my arms and down my chest and then all of the way off me. I was naked now, except for my dance belt and my ballet slippers.

"Drape pas de deux, legs extended," he commanded and turned me away from him and lifted me, my back against his chest, and I extended my legs, knees bent, out to the side in graceful ballet pose. I was trembling, though, knowing what we were building up to, trying to control myself and to remain in traditional ballet positions at all times and to move into them and from them as gracefully as possible. I knew this was all part of the audition.

He had one arm around my belly, holding me to his chest, and his other hand was gliding below the waistband of my dancing belt. He started fondling my cock and balls and his lips went to the hollow of my neck. And I began to moan for him.

In smooth movements, he unsnapped my dance belt and let it fall to the floor and pushed the waist of his leotard down below his ball sack.

"Ankles on the back of my thighs," he whispered in a hoarse voice, and I brought my legs around his and hooked them above the back of his knees. He lifted me then and settled my channel on his already-condom-clad engorged cock, and he was raising and lowering me on his tool, fucking me as I groaned and moaned for him. He wasn't large, but he was long, and it was all I could do to maintain graceful ballet positions and not shudder or writhe to his strongly controlled, slow, deep fuck. He was murmuring and I could hear him crying softly. I felt he was worshipping my body as he fucked me—and that he was savoring every deep penetration as if it was his last—which I realized, and he must too, it very possibly would be.

He wasn't steady enough on his feet to do this for very long. He pulled me off his cock and, sharply instructing me not to break position, hobbled over to the piano, carrying me in front of him. He gently lowered my buttocks to the piano keyboard and moved in between my legs. He slid his cock deeply inside me again, and then we were fucking in earnest, my buttocks making discordant music on the keyboard.

He was wheezing and breathing heavily, and I was afraid he was going to expire on the spot, but he also was whispering to me how good a fuck I was— and a very nice dancer too.

He wasn't particularly vigorous, but I gave him as good a ride as I could, and running my hands over the veins popping out on his torso and arms was arousing to me. I imagined that when he was younger and healthier he was quite a good lover.

I did what I could to convince him he was still a good lover, and he began to cry again at my acceptance of him moving inside me. I pulled his face down to mine and gave him a sweet kiss as I felt his pelvis jerk and the filling out of the bulb of the condom inside me. He was smiling in gratitude when we parted.

I started to whisper, "Did I—?"

"Monday morning at 9:30 sharp. Here and ready to dance," he murmured back at me.

And, with that, I became a member of the cast of *Defiance*.

* * * *

"Now? You want me to go with you now?"

"Sure, now," Gil said to me. He was smiling and holding up a picnic basket. "This food's not going to be in very good condition the next time Masters and Handelsman are gone for half a day without expecting us to tag along."

"But I've got to practice," I said. "I got a place in the dance troupe."

"So I gathered," Gil said. He gave me a funny look, but I had no idea why. And then he continued on. "You don't think there's any way Cersenka's going to fire you from the troupe, is there?"

I surveyed his face for evidence of censure. I'm sure he knew what I had to do for Cersenka to get the job. But he probably didn't know that I'd already become a favorite of Cersenka's and was being taken frequently in the dressing room he occupied at the theater.

Catching my expression, Gil stammered out, "I mean we're too close to the opening for him to replace you, aren't we? And . . . and I've seen you dance. I don't think there's any chance he'll want to replace you."

"But where will we go?" I then asked, anxious to change the subject. "A picnic on the dock, watching the *Boxoffice,* won't be much fun."

"I've got wheels," he said, "And a map and an assurance that there's a slice of rural paradise within a three-quarter's hour drive."

"Wheels?" I asked skeptically?

94

"Come, come with me," Gil said as he reached his hand out to me, tilted his head, and gave me a winning smile. "Come with me and I'll take all of your cares away, if only for an afternoon."

How could I resist? I went into the men's room off the lobby and stripped off the unitard I was wearing when he stopped me en route to the dance rehearsal hall. Gil stood in the doorway, leaning up against the doorframe and giving me a little smile. I felt like blushing. Here I was being fucked at least once a day and by different men, feeling so jaded and used, and yet I was blushing when I noticed a man watching me undress. Of course Gil wasn't like any of the others. He'd said he wanted me, sure, but he hadn't been pushy yet. And thus far I hadn't been with him. And he was the most arousing to me of the bunch.

"What?" I asked over my shoulder as I pulled the unitard off and turned my head to catch the expression on my face.

"Can you turn, please, and face me? Just a moment?"

I did and stood as tall as I could, my arms out to my side. Gil's eyes slitted and I could hear the raspy breath escaping him.

"God, you're beautiful. Can I . . . can we . . .?"

"No picnic?" I asked, putting on a pouty face. "You promised me a picnic."

"I'll be outside in the hall," he said, his voice full of regret.

When he was gone, I put my T-shirt over my head and rolled it down my chest, and then I pulled up a pair of tight jeans. I didn't put on any briefs, and I turned toward the door in surprise when I heard another intake of breath and a low, "Oh, god." Gil was peering around the corner, and his eyes were riveted on my crouch as I slowly pulled my zipper up.

There was no question that Gil wanted me. He wasn't pushing me, though. I liked him all the more for that. And I was sort of sorry I'd cock teased him like that. I hadn't really decided whether I'd give myself to him today. I rather liked the suspense—and the thought that I had some decision in the matter as opposed to most of what had been happening to me of late.

"What? This car?" I asked as we reached the staff parking lot. "Isn't this the lighting technician's car . . . whatshisname's car?"

"Jack, the senior lighting technician. Yes, this is his Mustang. And you don't know what I had to do to get the use of it. But it was worth it. You need an afternoon away. You look more relaxed already."

I frowned, turning away from Gil so he wouldn't see me do it, and I felt bad then. I was pretty sure I knew what Gil had had to do to get use of the car. I'd seen him fucking the lighting technician. It had made me think at the time that he'd do almost anyone, that he had no taste or limits at all, but now I was mad at myself for jumping to that conclusion. Now it seemed likely he'd done it for me—to get use of this car to take me for a drive. Who would have guessed Gil was such a romantic? For me.

The first few miles driving out of D.C. were a little hairy. We missed the turn to the 14th Street Bridge that would have taken us across the Potomac at the Pentagon and had to find our way around the Tidal Basin and catch the Arlington Memorial Bridge that headed into Arlington Cemetery on the Virginia side. Gil managed to get off on the George Washington Memorial Parkway, headed west, though, and within minutes we were in parkland running up the Potomac on the Virginia side and I was feeling freer and less pressed already.

"What are we in this rut for, anyway?" Gil asked as we rode west under towering trees.

"Is that a rhetorical question?" I asked. And then when he didn't respond immediately, I tried a couple of answers. "Because we just fell into it and can't seem to climb out? Or because we like the fucking?"

Gil laughed at that. "No, seriously."

I thought for a few minutes and then tried again. "Because of the rush it gives us—well, me, at least. The theater is my life. It excites me. And it puts me beside so much talent."

"Like the lion of the theater, Creighton Masters, who hides behind your writing skills?" Gil asked. His voice was softer now. He was being serious now.

"His talent *is* mammoth," I answered. "It will come back. The success of *Defiance* will get him going again."

"A success built on your writing? You virtually wrote *Defiance*, didn't you?"

I didn't answer; I looked out over the Potomac and trained my eyes on a couple of scull shells practicing racing below the gray-rock walls of Georgetown University.

"Who named it *Defiance*?"

The sculls were almost neck and neck. I couldn't decide which one of them I wanted to draw ahead. It was frustrating not knowing who to pull for—not having decided to pick which scull I perceived to be the eventual winner or to invest my wishes in the underdog.

"You named it that, didn't you? It's in the name itself. Can't you see that part of you was screaming to be free of this?"

I heard calls from the girls in back of both of the sculls, voiced almost simultaneously, and the sculls, still neck and neck, lost power. I sighed my profound disappointment that they both had given up, not establishing a winner.

"OK. Let's return to Masters. What if he doesn't come back? What if he has no plays in him anymore?" Gil said. I didn't answer. "Is the power of his cocking enough then?"

"I don't know, Gil," I said, turning toward him in anger. "Is the power of his cock good enough for you?"

"Ouch," Gil responded. But he failed to rise in anger. He gave me a lopsided smile instead. "I repeat . . . if his talent doesn't come back?"

"I don't know," I answered after the Mustang had churned away another mile upstream.

"What would you do if you were free to just go away from here?" he asked.

"I don't think about that," I answered.

"That's one reason for us to go on this little excursion . . . to think outside the box. The box represented by Arena Stage, the boxes our individual masters have made for us."

"Only one reason?" I asked.

"Of course not," he flashed back. "You know the other reason."

"Yeah, I guess?"

"And are you scared?"

"No, I guess not," I answered. "But I also don't know, Gil. Are you just going to take me like everyone else has—just because you want me? Or am I going to be given choices?"

"Check," Gil said, and I was glad that he at least attempted a smile. "Did anyone ever tell you you were a very clever boy?" he finished with.

"Not recently," I answered. And for some reason that answer made me sad. And then I went back on the topic we'd slipped off of. "I don't think of Arena Stage as a box. I love the theater. I'd want to stay in it. Maybe not here in Washington, maybe not even in New York. Maybe I'd want to do something fresh out on the West Coast."

"What's in the cards for you and Masters after *Defiance*?" he asked.

"I don't know," I answered. "I'll have to try to get him to cut down on the spending, of course. And there's another play."

"Another play? He's written another play."

"Well, not exactly."

"Ah, I see. *You've* written another play for him."

"Yeah, I guess so."

"So, can I read this play when we get back?"

"Yeah, I guess so." And then I wanted him to do some answering. "So, your turn. Where will you go? What would you do if you left here?"

"I'd go far, far away. Maybe even to the West Coast too. If I didn't leave Lenny pissed, I probably could get a job in the entertainment industry out there. Maybe not plays. But TV or movies, maybe. I'm good as a fixer now. And I am workin' on gettin' away. I've got my escape fund building."

"Your escape fund?"

"Yeah, that's what I call it," Gil answered, and then he gave a little nervous laugh.

"And how much more do you need before you can escape?" I asked.

"Hmmm. I don't know."

"How will you know when you have enough then?" I asked.

He didn't respond, so I continued, "Maybe until you decide how much you really need, you're just not all that anxious to escape."

We rode in silence for the last couple of miles in a wealthy rural area, with mansions buried behind natural woodland growth, until we got where Gil had told me we were headed—the Virginia side of Great Falls Park, bordering the stretch of rapids on the Potomac several miles above Washington, D.C.

When we drove into the parking area, it was almost deserted. It was early in the year, and no one could have anticipated in advance that we'd have such a glorious, warm day. Gil parked at the far edge of the lot, under a tree.

He turned to me, a wary expression on his face. "This is where I tell you I want you and wait to see how you react."

"Maybe differently than before," I answered in a small voice.

"Differently enough?"

"Yes . . . maybe."

Gil had his arm around my neck. He pulled me to him and we kissed. And while we were kissing, his hands were busy. He pulled my T-shirt over my head and was running his big, brown hands around my chest, pinching at my nipples with one hand, while the other slid down my belly and under the waistband of my jeans. He had undone my jeans snap, and I felt and even thought I could hear my zipper slowly descend as he ran his fingers into my pubic hair and pushed out with the back of his hand. I sighed at the feel of his fingers in my pubic hair, and then his hand descended lower and wrapped itself around my cock. His thumb flicked on my piss slit while my cock engorged and straightened out inside his fist.

I moaned and spread my legs, putting one foot up on the dashboard where it met the side window and the other one over his knee. He was slowly working my cock.

"Gil," I gasped, as I came up for air. He raised my arm that was pulled into his chest and lowered his face and buried his lips into my pit.

"Let me get over there in your seat, under you," He murmured, when he turned his head from tonguing my pit.

"No, Gil. No, please."

"Let me fuck you. I want to fuck you so bad," Gil moaned.

"Gil, I'm scared. You're so big in every way. You'll split me. Masters . . . Masters, he . . ."

"Shush, Sean. Shush. It will be fine. It will be good. I'll be gentle. We'll go slow. I wouldn't do anything to hurt you. Oh, god, let me fuck you. I want you so bad."

"No, not here," I said through clinched teeth and between gasps. "Let's go have the picnic and be more comfortable when we do it."

"But you want me. You want me, don't you?"

"Yes," I whispered. "Yes," I said louder. "But I'll still want you after the picnic lunch you brought along." I was still unsure, however. I didn't know how I'd react when we finally started doing it. I wanted him, but I had lied to him. I was, in fact, scared. I didn't want to fall for him. I was having trouble handling the men I had to take. I just didn't know. But I thought when push came to shove and I said I couldn't go through with it, he wouldn't force me. That already put him high on my list.

After that I let Gil take the lead. He took the picnic basket in one hand and my hand in the other, and we walked down the path along the side of the rapids until Gil decided to move off the path over toward a rock outcropping, where he found a private little tree-lined dell sheltered from the path by the rocks and carpeted in thick moss.

The setting was idyllic, amazing, actually, knowing it was this close to downtown D.C., and the sound of the rushing water over the rapids was soothing. I relaxed on the blanket through the picnic lunch, and the couple of beers we each had. We didn't discuss anything deep, not like the raw nerve endings we'd toyed with during the car ride. I said little, lying there in Gil's arms while we were sipping at our second beers. I hadn't put my T-shirt back on since the encounter in the Mustang, and Gil took his time working my chest with his hands and lips and removing my jeans as we lay there, and then I sighed and moaned while he fondled my cock and balls and fingered my channel entrance while we were kissing and he moved his lips to my nipples and pits.

While he was kissing me and working me, I was becoming scared again—not because I didn't want him, but because I was afraid I wanted him too much and because this would add yet another dimension to an already complicated situation—and because of that bulge in his trousers. I murmured that maybe we shouldn't be doing this, but Gil shushed me and assured me it would be fine and that this was exactly what we should be doing.

When he felt me relax to him, he rose and stood over me and slowly stripped down. I began moaning as soon as I saw his strong, heavily muscled, low-hung body—the first time I'd seen him in the altogether. A hulking black beauty, all power and primeval attraction.

There were no more questions, though. I no longer cared if he split me asunder. I turned on my back and spread my legs for him and he came down and covered my body with his. His massive cock was rubbing on my belly as he kissed me on the lips, and I needed nothing more than this to be set aflame. He felt my surrender in his kiss, and he started kissing and tonguing down my body.

When he reached the tip of my cock with his lips, I arched my back and murmured that he didn't need to do this.

"Yes, yes, I do," he answered in a husky voice. "This is important to me. This means something to me."

And then he made slow, sensual love to my cock and balls with his mouth and tongue. I raised my pelvis to him and began a slow motion with my hips when he had fully taken me in.

I'd never had attention paid to my cock and balls for this long and this well. I felt my seed rising in me, and I murmured that we'd better stop, that I might come. But he paid no attention to me. He kept sucking at my cock, putting pressure on it and scraping it with his teeth, coaxing me to give myself, my essence, to him. I was close, crying out that we needed to stop, that I wanted him inside me. But he was relentless. I grabbed for his head, burying my fingers in his hair, trying, without successful to pull his head away from me, fearful that the increased pumping of my hips would be too much for him to handle. But it wasn't too much for him to handle. I moved my legs over his shoulders and hugged his head close with my thighs. His fingers were digging deep inside my channel.

I knew I was being vocal, and I tried to tone myself down. But nothing like this had ever happened to me before. I was in full force in fucking his mouth. And now I wasn't trying to pull his head away, I was holding him close to me. I felt my balls being ingested into his mouth along with my cock and being moved to his cheeks on each side, and he began to hum, the vibrations driving me crazy and pushing . . . me . . . over the edge in a torrent that matched the race of the churning waters in the nearby Potomac.

He released me then and sat up over me and looked down at me with the most loving, tender look in his eyes. I lay under him, exhausted and panting, and looking up with an expression that mirrored his. I was horrified and exhilarated all at once. I loved him. That was the last thing I should be doing. But I couldn't hide it from myself, even if I could try to hide it from him. I was hopelessly in love with Gil Johnson.

He was on the move again, lifting my buttocks with his strong brown hands and rolling my pelvis. His lips went to my channel entrance, and I reached a whole new level of arousal as he tongue fucked me.

After that, when he covered my body with his and slowly, stopping as I found necessary, panting to open to him, to accommodate his gigantic size, slid his cock into my channel. As he promised, he possessed me slowly, moving massively inside me, giving me the sensation of doors opening willingingly, welcomingly to him and walls stretching, sighing their love and crying out their jubilation in the progress of his possessing cock, bringing me to ejaculation again while he was still inching to the center of me. There was little pain even though he was so long and thick. And then, totally sheathed, he began to move in and out me, as every nerve in my body ran to luxuriate in the full possession of me by that moving, mastering cock. But as nice as his slow, easy, eternal fucking was, it was almost a sideshow to that glorious blow job Gil had given me.

* * * *

Three weeks later, the production was coming together. The script rewrites were finished, which was a good thing, because most of my time was now spent in dance rehearsals. And the dance routines were also about as close to perfection as they were going to get.

Masters was brooding, no longer the center of attention, and spent much of the time during the day in the townhouse, going through papers he wouldn't let

105

me see. Often at night he was on the *Boxoffice,* however, and those nights he came home too exhausted to mess with me when he got into bed. I knew that this was something Gil was doing—for me. He was occupying both Masters and Handelsman, and keeping them off me.

It also meant, however, that the occasions when Gil and I could meet were rare. But meet we did, where we could. And we made love whenever there was an opportunity.

Although Gil was helping to minimize the demands on me from Masters and Handelsman, there was little he could do with Miloslav Cersenka. I had become the dance master's favorite. He frequently would call me into his room at the theater after dance practices and would fuck me on the chaise lounge there.

I worried about him, though. The closer the dance sequences were coming to perfection, the more ravished his body appeared. He was dragging to the rehearsals in the end, and he was asking me to show the other dancers what he meant when he was trying to correct their positions. His eyes took on a haunted look, and his fucking was labored and almost perfunctory, even though he cried through each one as if it was his last.

Thus, it was bound to happen on that day, when, face flushed and excitement bursting out of him, Cersenka ended a dance rehearsal by saying we were ready. He trumpeted the fact that he had fulfilled his responsibilities a good week before the dress rehearsal and while Handelsman was still yelling at his actors and calling them fucking dumb donkeys.

He took me by the arm and led me to his room, bubbling over with pride at just how perfect the dance sequences were. As I stripped for him, I could hear him behind me, wheezing, but still talking up a storm, barely intelligible and slurring his words, although I knew he was congratulating himself on cheating death—on having taken on another production, prepared another dance ensemble, when everyone, all of his doctors included, had warned him it was too much. How he had snatched his victory and produced a masterpiece of dance work.

He died in my arms, his cock inside me, his face buried in the hollow of my neck. He jerked, and I thought he was coming. But, he wasn't. He was going.

I dressed him and sat him up at the dressing table, as if he had slumped over dead there. Then I dressed myself and went to the front of the theater and told them I'd found him unconscious in his room and that they should call 911.

The sounds of the sirens were coming closer as I left Arena Stage through the lobby entrance and crossed Maine Avenue for the short walk to the 7th Street townhouse.

Masters was sitting at the desk in the living room, looking through some papers. I walked over to where he was sitting and looked down and recognized envelopes from a Realtor in New York City and saw at once that they concerned the sale of our apartment in Manhattan.

He swept other papers over those, but he hadn't been fast enough. I'd seen them. And I was in shock. But as I'd already been in shock, the import of the papers didn't occur to me until later.

Masters looked up at me, a wary, guilty look on his face.

"You're back early," he said.

"Miloslav Cersenka is dead," I said. I knew I sounded flat, too matter of fact. That's what shock was doing to me. "Just now. I found him in his room. I suppose those sirens we're hearing are for him."

"Had he finished preparing the dances for *Defiance*?" Masters asked. No "Oh my God," no "Oh, I'm sorry you had to be the one to find him," no "I'm sorry we pushed him like that," no "What a great loss to the theater." Just, "Had he finished his part of my fucking play?"

I had never hated Creighton Masters as much as I did at that moment.

Chapter Seven: Final Curtain

Dress rehearsal for *Defiance* was exhausting—for me, at least, since I had to dance in it. But I'm sure it was nerve-wracking for Masters and Handelsman, too, because this was their last crack at making it right before the drama critics descended on them. They were so pumped up on reviewing and celebrating and agonizing over minutia on the production that they went straight to Handelsman's yacht, the *Boxoffice*, in the yacht basin near the theater. And Masters told me I had to come along.

Before we left the theater, I called the Gangplank restaurant, which was close to closing time, and cajoled them into preparing a late supper to send over to the yacht for the two men. I myself wasn't hungry. I was just exhausted. And after I'd accepted the meals at the gangplank to the yacht and taken them into the salon, where the two men barely noticed they were even there they were so animated and excited, I sat back into the cushions of the curved bench lining the fantail of the yacht. I brought my legs up onto the cushion, stretched out, and gave myself up to sleep.

I couldn't go to sleep, though. I was exhausted beyond sleep. I shut my eyes tightly and tried controlled breathing, but it just didn't happen. It was both a bad thing and a good thing that I couldn't go to sleep. First came the bad thing.

Masters and Handelsman must have assumed I'd gone to sleep, because they made no attempt to moderate their discussion.

"So, you've done it, have you?" Handelsman said.

"Yes, the apartment's sold and I'm having the clothes sent up to your place in Connecticut," Masters said.

My ears perked up. I hadn't heard anything about this sale—although I'd found he was trying to sell his apartment—no, our apartment. I lived there too.

"And you're sure you're done with it?" Handelsman said.

"Yes," I heard Masters speak. "I didn't much care for it anyway. As long as I had Lawrence for those earlier plays—and Sean now—the attention was pleasant, but those empty years between the time Lawrence died and I took on Sean were frustrating. I'm happily done with it. Your invitation to come live out my days with you couldn't have come at a better time."

"And to think that no one in the theater ever knew who was writing your plays."

"That was part of the pleasant part," Masters said. And then he laughed. "Such a joke on all those pompous theater people."

"Including me," Handelsman said.

"Oh, no, never including you, Lenny. You were special. There's never been anyone like you."

"And Sean?" Handelsman said, followed by his own laugh. "What will we do with sweet young Sean up in Connecticut?"

"Oh, I'm sure we'll think of something," Masters answered. "You know how we shared Gil. Sean has charms of his own. So small and yielding. I wonder how he'd do with doubling. Gil wouldn't stand for that. But Sean will do anything I tell him to do." His voice suddenly sounded husky, and I opened my eyes, lifted my head, and peered into the salon through the window. The two were sitting close together, and Handelsman had one hand inserted in Masters' shirt front and the other was stroking Masters' exposed cock.

"Shall we retire to the cabin?" Handelsman said in a hoarse voice.

"Yes, I think so," Masters answered.

"And Sean, shall we wake him and take him with us?"

"Later," Masters answered. And then they both rose and, laughing and joking, embraced and entered the corridor leading back to the staterooms.

I could hardly wait for them to be gone. I was suddenly alert and believed if I didn't get off the yacht and away instantly, I would begin to hyperventilate. My whole world was shattering. What a complete bastard Masters was. And Handelsman wasn't far behind.

I slipped off the yacht and loped blindly up the grassy embankment. I had to find Gil. I needed Gil—now more than ever before. Where could he be? One place was a good bet—adding to his escape fund. I started walking briskly toward the elevated Southwest Freeway, both what I had just heard and the brisk evening breeze making so much clear to me now.

* * * *

"Am I interrupting anything?"

I turned and was surprised to see Sean standing next to me at the bar in the Bachelor Pad gay club. He looked more like his favorite uncle had just died than that he been part of an almost-flawless dress rehearsal for a production we had all been slaving on for months.

"What's the matter, Sean?" I asked. "You look sorta like shit."

"I said, am I interrupting anything, Gil?" he repeated. His eyes were flashing and his nostrils were flaring, and he looked like he was thinking of picking a fight with me.

"Just a drink, Sean," I answered. "I haven't been in here for any other purpose since before we took that car ride up to Great Falls. I wouldn't do that to you." I reached out and put my hand on his forearm. He was trembling like a high-strung racehorse.

"Sorry, Gil," he whispered, and he just sort of collapsed on the stool next to me. "I've just . . . I can't . . . oh, shit."

"Come, let's go back to the townhouse," I said. "We'll have privacy there, and you can tell me what the matter is."

But when we got back to the townhouse, Sean didn't speak. He was at me like a bitch in heat, crawling up my leg and rubbing his chest against mine, and unzipping my jeans and digging for my cock.

I decided, without any trouble, that talk could come later, and I picked him up in my arms and mounted the stairs and gently laid him on the bed. He moaned as I undressed him and he cried out as I knelt between his legs and started making love to his cock and balls and hole and not stopping, not letting up, until he had given me what I wanted, his total release. Then I stood and held his legs out wide by the ankles and mounted him, this time in a swift thrust that almost lifted him off the bed and made him cry to the ceiling. I rode him hard and deep to my own ejaculation, skin on skin, no niceties, full commitment. He cried for me like an animal in heat, digging his nails and the heels of his feet into my butt cheeks and holding me close inside him and yelling crudities of the fuck that I had no idea he even knew.

We were stretched out on the bed, in an embrace, when he broke down and started to cry.

"What is it, Sean?" I whispered. "What has you worked up? The play is great. Your dancing was great. It made me harden right up. I'm glad you came looking for me to fix that."

This didn't brighten him up a bit. I never was much of a comedian.

"Come on, you can tell me."

"A sham, all a sham," Sean whispered. I was relieved that I'd started him talking about it.

"What was a sham?"

"Masters. Just a big fake."

I laughed. I couldn't help it. "Of course he is. That was always apparent—to anyone who bothered to look."

"You don't understand, Gil," he said. "He didn't write any of those great plays. The guy he had living with him before, Lawrence, the guy who was killed in the automobile accident a couple of years before Masters hired me—he wrote his plays for him. I can see that now, he hired me just to write his plays for him. This Lawrence guy was the one who wrote his earlier plays. The only plays Masters wrote himself were the ones that didn't work."

"Doesn't surprise me," I answered. "But speaking of plays, Sean. I read your latest one. It's brilliant. It's gonna be a hit."

"Thanks, Gil, I needed to hear that," Sean said. He sat up beside me and leaned his face down to mine and we kissed. When he rose back from the kiss, he looked more in control now, and the sadness had evaporated from his eyes.

"And I overheard him and Handelsman talking on the yacht. They are going to Handelsman's place in Connecticut after this. They are moving us to Connecticut."

"Ain't no way I'm fuckin' movin' to Connecticut," I muttered.

"And Masters is giving up the sham of writing plays. He said he'd never been interested in that anyway—he just liked living off the playwrighting talents of others. He's just a big fraud. And he's retiring to Connecticut to live with Handelsman. What are we going to do, Gil?"

"Didn't you hear me?" I said. "There's no fucking way I'm going to Connecticut."

"But—"

"Or you either, if you are thinking straight," I continued. "What held in you thrall to Masters, Sean? You said you loved him. What about him did you love?"

He sat there, looking confused. Then his face cleared. "I loved him because he was the lion of the

114

theater," Sean said. "Because of his writing talent. Because I believed in his writing talent."

"Which is what, Sean?"

"All a sham," Sean whispered.

"Exactly. Can you hear your lion go meow now?"

For the first time that evening Sean laughed. And it was a good, throaty laugh. I guess I wasn't as much of a loss as a comic as I thought I was.

"And what do you need Masters for now, Sean?"

"Nothing."

"Did you hear and understand what I said about your play script? It's great. It's a winner. I've been working with Handelsman in the theater long enough to know a winner when I read one. We could take it to Broadway. But I suggest we take it to the West Coast. We both said that's where we'd go if we could follow our dream. There's work and a life for us both out there—together, if you'll have me."

Sean wasn't slow in giving me a definitive answer on that. He rolled me to my back and mounted my pelvis, holding my cock as he descended on it, and he fucked my cock until he'd come on my belly and I'd reciprocated deep inside him.

"Pack quickly," I whispered when our breathing had returned to normal again and we lay in each other's embrace. "We can be out of here and on our way in a half an hour."

"The play—*Defiance*. Opening night tomorrow," he murmured, and I was pleased to hear the regret in his voice. "And your escape fund."

"You were right about my escape fund," I said, with a low laugh. "I've had more than enough money saved for some time. I just needed a greater reason to leave than to stay. You're my reason. And, as far as the play, what do they do when someone's sick one night?"

"We can adjust the dances for one, or even two, missing," Sean answered.

"So, you're sick," I said. "Permanently sick. Sick of walking behind Masters and Handelsman and cleaning their asses for them. I mean, what's the fucking play mean to you now? Other than that you wrote it. It's tainted by Masters' shit. You've got another play here that will launch you out of his shadow. What's the play *Defiance* to us now, other than a symbol of our own defiance—of us sticking it back at Masters and Handelsman at last?"

"Nothing. Nothing, I guess." Sean answered. And there was none of the indecision in his voice that came out in his words. That had been my one worry. That, knowing *Defiance* was more his play than Masters'—much more—that maybe he couldn't just leave it, even knowing we were done here. That we'd been done here for some time; that we'd just been wallowing in a rut.

"Let's us get out of here, then." I was up already and half way to the shower.

"How, Gil?" Sean said, with a laugh. "We're both city boys in the city. Are we going to try to hitch across the country?"

"Nope, we're going in my new Mustang," I said. And I grinned. This may be the first inkling that Sean would have that this plan wasn't all that impromptu. He had fallen into my own already-formed plans perfectly. "Not a new Mustang, but mine—ours—now. Bought it off the lighting technician guy. Hoped you'd

116

relent and let me fuck you in it one day. And maybe you will. It's a long way by road to L.A. from D.C. How's that sound, Sean?"

"Best offer I've had in a long, long time."

~

About the Author

Habu is one of the pen names of a former supersonic spy jet pilot, intelligence agent, male model, movie actor, and diplomat. A wild youth in South East Asia was spent enjoying whatever sexual opportunities came his way, and much of his gay male writing is about recalling incidents from those days and inventing ones he'd perhaps have liked to experience. He now leads a very quiet and ordinary happily married family life.

An American, he is a published mainstream novelist and short story writer under another name and in another dimension of his life. He has written or cowritten (with Sabb) approaching 1,000 published short stories and over 100 published erotica e-books, primarily of gay fiction but also memoir, straight fiction and ménage fiction. His hand and creative writing can be seen in stories and books by habu, sr71plt, Dirk Hessian, Shabbu, and Stephen Kessel—among unrevealed others that might surprise readers. The fictionalized GM memoir *Flying High, Diving Deep* is loosely based on his life experiences. He can be found at the adults only gay male site www.BarbarianSpy.com, which he shares with Sabb and Dirk Hessian.

Our authors always like to receive feedback, and appreciate it when readers post reviews at distributors and other sites.

BarbarianSpy

FOR LITERARY HEAT

Not all books listed below may currently be on release.
* indicates the book is available in paperback and e-book.

BOOKS BY DIRK HESSIAN

Xtreme Erotica
The King's Men
Shores of Tripoli
Prophecy of Noto
Pretender's Fate

General Erotica/Romance
Fire Down the Valley*
Constantinople*
The Beautiful Way*
Blue and Gray
Colonel's Treasure
Beginning of Time
Labyrinth

BOOKS BY HABU

Gay Erotica

Memoir Faction
Flying High, Diving Deep*

Xtreme Erotica
Apyko: The Greek Pimp
Visits of the Schlange
Second Coming: Emile La Cour Unleashed
Vortex: Sacrificed by Curiosity*
Dark Angel Sounding *(in e-book & included in
Sounding:Ultimate Control Paperback)**
Sounding: Ultimate Control (*Print Only*)*
Sounding Five *(in e-book & included in
Sounding:Ultimate Control paperback)**

General Erotica
Romance

Arena Stage
Trading Partners (Valentine's Day)
Friday Nights with Lenny (Christmas Romance)
Snowy, Snowy Nights (Christmas Romance)
Four Coins
Lower Than the Heart (Valentine's Day)
Brambleton
Gotta Keep Trying
Finding Amnad
Platres Conclave
Other Novels/Novellas
Cruising Gigolo (bisexual)
Prepared in Cape Verdi
Gilded Cage
House on Park
Anything for Ambition
Dance of the Ravishers
Hard Knocks U*
My Neighbor's Spa*
Man's Man: Tales of a High Priced Gay Hooker*
Trip Money
Clint Folsom Mysteries Compendium Volume 1*
Death to Blonds - Stolen Judgment (Clint Folsom
Mystery)*
Clint Folsom Mysteries Compendium Volume 2*
The Indian Doctor
Sailorboy
Home to Fire Island
Choke Hold
Gay Erotica Anthologies
Fifty Seventy
Spy Tails 001*
Spy Tails 002*
Doubled*
Doubled Again*
Tails in the Tropics*
Tails in the Med*
Tails in the West*

Rough Riders*
Grab Bag 1*
Grab Bag 2*
Grab Bag 3*
Grab Bag 4*
Grab Bag 5*
Beyond the Beaded Curtain*
Habu's Christmas Balls
The Sporting Life*
Fetish Galore!*
Literary Gay Erotica
Cairo Surrender*
The Handyman*
Homeward Bound
Journey to Mirage*
Menage Erotica
Cruising Gigolo
13 Ways for Halloween
Luther*
The Indian Prince
Literary GLBT Fiction
Summer of Denial
BOOKS BY SHABBU
Velvet Interrogation
Finding Jason
Dirty Pool
Operation Black Jade
Cigars!*
Angel in the Barn
Gayly Complicated*
Despoiling David
The Tree of Idleness*
I Met a Man
Rough Road to Happiness
BOOKS BY SABB
Hiring in Hollywood
The Legend of Holleystone Grange
Surprise Encounters

She is He
Wrong Man
Loyal to his King
Barbarian Tales - Book One - Traveler's Tales*
Barbarian Tales - Book Two - Journeys Begin*
Barbarian Tales - Book Three - The Inheritance*
Barbarian Tales - Book Four - Road to Persepolis*